THE COLOUR OF FEAR

There should have been no difficulty in frightening a young lady into changing her evidence about a hit and run accident. However, David Mallin finds that too many people are interested in what may not have been an accident after all, and the young lady has unexpected support in reserve. Very soon, the only one frightened is Dave himself!

Books by Roger Ormerod
in the Linford Mystery Library:

A GLIMPSE OF DEATH
TIME TO KILL
FULL FURY
A SPOONFUL OF LUGER
SEALED WITH A LOVING KILL

ROGER ORMEROD

THE COLOUR OF FEAR

Complete and Unabridged

LINFORD
Leicester

First published in Great Britain

First Linford Edition
published April 1994

British Library CIP Data

Ormerod, Roger
   The colour of fear.—Large print ed.—
Linford mystery library
I. Title II. Series
823.914 [F]

ISBN 0–7089–7487–2

Published by
F. A. Thorpe (Publishing) Ltd.
Anstey, Leicestershire

Set by Words & Graphics Ltd.
Anstey, Leicestershire
Printed and bound in Great Britain by
T. J. Press (Padstow) Ltd., Padstow, Cornwall

This book is printed on acid-free paper

1

THE one with the black leather jacket and brown leather face was riding the bonnet, while the other eight of them tried to turn over the car. But a 3½ litre Rover is a heavy car, and they didn't even get a tyre from the ground. I was clinging to the steering wheel. There was no actual physical danger, but their howls were fiendish and their faces glowed with that gleeful venom that only the unbridled young can achieve.

My left arm still ached. The jockey turned to observe my distress through the windscreen. He looked like a shaggy ox. Then he pressed his face against the glass and jeered, spreading his sprawling features terrifyingly. It was not an experience I would cherish. I could do very little to retaliate, but I put on the wipers, though they only brushed his nose aside. Then I sprayed him with window cleaner. Nothing changed on his face; it didn't get any cleaner. But something unpleasant came into his eyes.

Up to then it had all been youthful exuberance, a gentle warning, but it was poised only a gesture away from viciousness. I decided it was time to get out of there. The engine was still ticking over. I revved it. The howls became screams of anger and the rocking more vigorous, but I slipped the automatic to drive and let the car drift forward. Then I did an abrupt U-turn. I wasn't moving fast; nothing spectacular. The big sable slob slid from the bonnet, but the yelp was in colloquial English, so I must have run over somebody else's toe.

Then I was in the clear. I slowed and looked back. Nobody was running after me. Toni was standing on the steps of the house. I think she was laughing. The oaf in the leather jacket was sitting in the road. He was certainly laughing.

2

But I couldn't forget those eyes.

For the second time I was glad I had borrowed Elsa's Rover; they'd have had my little Porsche on its back in a couple of minutes. But instinct had told me to bring the bigger car. You can't get an active young woman into a low sports car in a busy street, not if she's reluctant. And there had been reason to believe she would be.

Her name was Toni Brent. About nineteen I'd say, small and dark and fiery, and, as far as I could tell, not in the least frightened by me. Well, she should have been. For a week I'd been hovering around like a menacing rain cloud, and all I'd got had been a raised eyebrow and what seemed very like a giggle. Perhaps I'm not sufficiently menacing.

It had all come to a damp climax the night before. The rain had started while I'd been waiting outside the art college where she was taking sculpture. She came out as always with a skip to indicate freedom, a glance at the sky

3

to welcome it, and a toss of her head to dismiss the weather. I was using the Porsche that day, and I'd left it parked in the square, because she never did anything but go home. So I followed her on foot.

From time to time I allowed her to turn and see me. I had my slouch trilby, pulled well down in an attitude of aggression, and my Bogart raincoat. I kept my hands in the pockets, inferring that one of them might be grasping something offensive. By that time she ought to have been nervous. But she had been treating me as though I could be a shy suitor, enraptured by her figure and personality. Mind you, both were worth consideration, but at a less urgent moment.

I decided it was about time we spoke together. I mean, she ought to realize what she was up against. It seemed a pity to tear her bright and carefree life to shreds, but that's what it's all about. When you're paid for it.

But simultaneously she apparently

4

decided that she'd had enough of me and suddenly burst ahead with a clatter of heels, and I couldn't catch her before she reached the house.

That square is the most depressing area I have ever patrolled. At one time it had probably been a graceful circle of three-storey dwellings, on the edge of town and quietly basking in anonymity around a central island of lawn and trees. But now it was a bus terminus, the square asphalted over as a car park, and with four bus stops round its perimeter. There's a lot of thought goes into planning bus stops. If you can find a draughty space, it's ideal. If it's not draughty, knock down a few buildings to let the wind through, and slaughter anything green in case it suppresses the diesel stench. So now there were only two of those houses still standing at the blank end, and two dismal street-lamps with chill blue light, and the odd miserable queue of passengers waiting in suspension for buses that came as a kind of afterthought, their bulk briefly shielding the wind now that it was too late.

Toni lived in one of the two houses. I was not aware of the circumstances of her life, but I'd already spent a number of hours watching the house, and what I'd seen going in and coming out had not been inspiring. She herself always wore tatty slacks or jeans and a tasselled, hairy kind of windcheater, so I supposed she was on the fringe, but the rest of them seemed to have gone way out into permissive no-man's land. I'd counted eleven, sex not immediately apparent. No doubt they could tell. If they cared. Their only common characteristic was the sullen disparagement with which they viewed the world. But mainly they ignored the rest of us. Perhaps there was still hope for Toni; at least she'd noticed me.

That evening she tripped lightly up the four steps to the front door, into the hall, and that was the last I saw of her. Technique now required that I should lurk in the vicinity, but at that time, although it was dark, the car park was still packed and the bus queues were at their longest. You can't lurk in such bustling surroundings, so I went for a cup of tea and a currant bun.

By the time I got back it was quieter. Buses came and went and the parked cars gradually melted away, leaving the Porsche naked in the far corner. The square became quiet, and from the nearby slums crept the local kids, looking for whatever devilment they could inflict. They didn't seem to mind the weather; they discovered something different that they could pester — me. Mainly they popped out at me from time to time to jeer, not understanding my behaviour. Several times they had to be chased away from the Porsche before they committed something dastardly with a hammer and a two-inch nail one of them carried. But it passed the time, though bruising my dignity. Eventually they went away.

The rain became sleet. It was January and cold, and I'd had enough. But I stayed on. Sometimes I get stubborn, which usually happens when I'm cold and wet, and then I think: don't let it beat you, Dave. And also when there's something I can't understand, such as why I was supposed to be terrifying Toni Brent.

So I leaned against a lamp-post with my trousers soaked, and kept an eye on the window that I'd discovered was her bedroom. Gradually the cold seeped into my bones, but I was determined she should have one last glimpse of me before retiring, and the later that turned out to be, the more she would be impressed by my determination. It turned out to be a little after eleven. The last bus had left; my car was the only vehicle around. I was alone in the wet, and by then not at all sure I could move.

Then the light came on in the bedroom. The curtains remained closed. Nothing happened. I tried to light a soggy cigarette. The light went off, and what I had been waiting for happened.

An edge of the curtain moved aside. Only an inch, but enough. She was aware of me. I raised my head, allowed her to see my eyes — full of frightful warning — then the curtain closed.

I was free to go home. I levered myself from the lamp-post and walked stiffly over to the Porsche. It seemed a pity to dump my sodden bulk into its immaculate interior. I opened the door. There was a man sitting in the passenger's seat.

I got in. "Take you somewhere?" I asked politely.

"You could have watched from here," he said. "It's quite comfortable."

The blue light slanted in through his window, shadowing his face into sharper planes than would be normal. But even allowing for that there was a certain strained gauntness about him that didn't fit his age. He'd have been around twenty-eight, and was wearing a blue, short raincoat, no hat, but thin, hard gloves. He was fair, his eyes light, his jaw positive.

"If I'd wanted comfort," I said, "I'd have gone home. Who are you?"

He ignored that. "You're David Mallin, enquiry agent, late of the Birmingham City Police, and at present keeping under observation a young woman who happens to be a Crown witness." He smiled. It might have been a pleasant smile in warmer light.

"She also happens to be attractive," I pointed out. "I could be trying to date her."

"She's not your type."

"How can you know that?"

"I know your wife."

I looked again, and then I placed him. Blaine — no, Braine, that was it. A constable in my time. Lew Braine. We'd met, and yes, he could have known my ex-chief, Geoff Forbes, and known Geoff's wife, Elsa, before poor Geoff was killed. And, apparently, he knew that Elsa and I were now married.

"You're Lew Braine," I said.

He nodded. "And now we know

where we are, I'd like to ask you what you're really up to."

"There's no law against standing around in the sleet."

"There is if you're watching my witness."

"I haven't touched her, spoken to her . . ."

"You're frightening her."

"Do you really think so?" I asked with interest.

Then he laughed, shortly, perhaps briefly amused. "No. You're hopeless at it. Why not pack it in?"

"I'll run you home first."

"My own car's only round the corner."

"Then will you please get out of mine and let me go. I'm cold."

He unlatched the door and swung a foot out. Wetness gusted in. "The inspector's not going to like it, Mallin," he said. "Just keep out of this, eh? It's too big for you."

He got out, slammed the door, and gave an ironic salute.

"Goodnight, constable," I called, starting the engine.

"Sergeant," he shouted as I let in the clutch.

Then I departed for Shropshire. What was supposed to be too big for me? It was only supposed to be a hit-and-run case.

We were still living in the big house that was really Elsa's, though the cost of maintaining it was becoming a little worrying. I'd have moved happily nearer to Birmingham, but Elsa was clinging warmly to her home, and still kept Doris as her housekeeper. Doris was an expensive luxury, and anyway she didn't think much of David Mallin, but I'd never have suggested getting rid of her. Where would the old dear have gone? It was Doris who welcomed me home that night. No doubt she'd waited up, just to exercise that disapproving glare of hers. By that time the Porsche's heater had succeeded in cooking me nicely. I was like a steamed pudding, and maybe I didn't smell too good. Doris sniffed.

"You'll be wanting something to eat," she said, just hoping I'd say no so that her sandwiches would be wasted.

"Just dying. Has Elsa gone to bed?"

Elsa had not. She was sitting in the kitchen in pyjamas and a housecoat, reading Proust against a teapot, and eating my sandwiches. She looked up as I came in. By that time I'd got rid of the raincoat and hat, but my suit was visibly steaming.

"David," she said, "what nonsense have you been up to now?"

As you know, Elsa has never approved of my activities as an enquiry agent. We'd been married nearly a year, and she still maintained that we could manage very well on her personal investments. But recently she'd complained less when I disappeared for days on end, obviously realizing that my small contribution **to the household fund was becoming**

13

more important. Complained less, but had not become encouraging. She'd ventured a polite enquiry now and again, perhaps believing she ought to show interest. But on this case I'd offered her no hints, said absolutely nothing.

"I'll just go and get into something dry," I told her. "Leave a sandwich for me."

When I got down again they'd heated some soup, and my tea was laced with brandy. Not a wonderful combination. Doris was nodding, nodding, watching me with disapproval until Elsa sent her off to bed, and then Elsa made a tentative start.

"You must be quite mad," she said. "Is anything worth it, if you get pneumonia?"

"I used to do this sort of thing regularly, when I was in the police."

"But you can make your own choices, now you're out of it."

"Not always."

She considered that, lit a cigarette,

and frowned. "You mean you've got no choice?"

I nodded. "Something like that."

"David, is there something wrong?"

"Nothing wrong. Do you want any more of those sandwiches? It's just that sometimes you start on a case you can't drop, and the fact that it's January just makes it more uncomfortable."

Then she said something that quite startled me. "Is there any way I can help?"

I looked up. Her large, dark eyes were even wistful. You've got to understand about Elsa. She likes to conduct her life in a kind of ladylike, inoffensive fashion, pretending a gentle scorn for my earthy profession, but when it comes to it, I've found, she can join in with gay abandon and enjoy herself immensely. Well . . . any other case and I'd have said yes. But not this one.

"It's all that tiresome business of watching and waiting."

"Not some sordid divorce!" she cried in disgust.

"Nothing sordid at all," I assured her. "A court case, a witness, and perhaps an error in the evidence. All very paltry. It's just boring, that's all."

Or rather, had been until Det. Sgt. Lew Braine came into it. I tried not to frown as I bent over my cup of tea.

"And you'll be going out tomorrow?" she asked.

"Not until after lunch. Oh, I wondered if I could borrow the Rover."

"Of course." She closed Proust firmly. "Why?"

"It's more appropriate."

"For what you have in mind?"

"Yes." I offered nothing.

"Really, David, you can be quite exasperating," she said sharply, and she went off to bed.

By the time I was ready to leave the next day she hadn't spoken about it again. There was a distinct coolness, but I decided it was best not to disturb it, and simply asked her for the keys. She handed them over.

Between us we had three cars, my

Porsche, Elsa's 3½ litre Rover, and the Dolomite Sprint she'd bought as an economy gesture; as it would have been if she could have brought herself to part with the Rover. But it was still with us, and I was glad I'd got it when Toni came out of the art college. If I'd been younger and more sexy, maybe she'd have gone for the Porsche. But there's something very comforting about the big Rover, and one can only think the best of the driver of such a car. I'd got my other hat on, the curly-brimmed one, and a motoring coat. The general impression was supposed to be one of solid respectability.

It struck her as she clattered down the steps. She paused. After all I was parked in a restricted zone. I raised my hat, and swept open the door.

"I wonder if you'd like a lift home."

She considered me with her head on on side. "It's only a few minutes' walk."

"I know."

"Of course you do." She smiled.

"What's happened to your smashing little car?"

"It's at home. This is my wife's."

It put things firmly on a business footing. "Oh," she said.

"I wanted to talk."

"And so you should," she told me severely, and without further discussion she got in the car.

It was quite clear that my period of carefully laid-on frightening had not worked. As we started off she pointed out that we were going the wrong way, but otherwise she seemed unperturbed. She waited patiently for my explanation.

"My name is David Mallin," I said. "I'm an enquiry agent, and I've been employed to ask you to change your evidence about a certain car accident."

There was a pause. I glanced sideways, and she was looking at me with vague amusement. "Ask?" she said. "Simply ask?"

"At first."

"But why should I change it?"

"You may not have told the truth."

"But I did. I simply told the police what I saw. What would you like me to tell them?"

"That you saw something different."

"But how can I do that?" she asked, so sincerely that I knew I was in trouble right away. She didn't even know what a good, full-blooded lie was.

"You won't lose your way?" she asked anxiously.

"No, oh no."

I fed the car into a traffic stream. We were on the inner ring road.

"So you've asked," she said. "Now what?"

"Now I begin to persuade you."

"Which you intend to do by talking about money," she suggested.

"Yes. I now tell you that I've got a thousand pounds in cash in an envelope. Open the glove compartment in front of you."

She made no move. "I'll take your word," she said icily.

"That money was given to me to

use as I like," I told her. "I haven't touched it yet. If you're sensible and reasonable we can split it between us. Five hundred each."

"Have you got a cigarette?" she asked.

I gave her my pack and lighter, not taking my eyes off the bustling traffic. She bounced smoke from the windscreen.

"And if I tell you to keep your five hundred?" she asked.

"I offer more."

"As much as the whole thousand?" she said, smiling.

"If you'll agree. All you need to do is say you made a mistake — it wasn't that car. And then the money's yours."

"But that would leave nothing for you."

"It leaves the experience. Having met you. And knowing you're still alive and healthy," I said meaningly.

She laughed. It was a delightful little choke of laughter. "You're quite ridiculous," she said. "In the same statement you tell me that I might not continue to be healthy, and also that it's worth five hundred pounds to you simply to know I'm safe and well. How can you explain that? It's a contradiction."

"I don't have to explain it — but I will. If you don't agree to that proposal, then I'll have a full thousand to use, and a lot of misery can be bought for that. Your parents . . . "

"I'm an orphan."

"Then . . . your friends. You've got friends, at the house."

"You'd harm them?" she demanded, in disbelief.

"Not me. But I'd find people who would."

"And it would cost you a thousand pounds?"

"For the best at the job."

"Then you can't gain either way," she pointed out. "So why do you do it? You stand in the pouring rain for **hours, trying to frighten me, get bored** to tears waiting around for me to come out of the college, and you're going to get nothing out of it."

"Satisfaction."

"You'd be satisfied!" she cried. "People get beaten up, cut about, assaulted, just over a bit of silly evidence, and it'd give you satisfaction!"

"If I can persuade you, my job's done. Then no one will be hurt. That's satisfaction."

But she was too clever for me. She pounced on it. "So really you've got no intention of hiring thugs. All you're trying to do is frighten me."

"I was hoping that would be enough."

"Well it's not."

"I don't frighten you at all?"

She gave a little giggle. "I think you're rather cute."

"I did my best."

"I'm sure you did."

"I hope you'll remember that, later — that I did my best."

There was a slight change in her tone. "Later?"

"I admit I'm not much good as a frightener," I told her. "It takes years of experience, really. But I was hoping to succeed, because if I fail I'll have to report back. And then they'll dispense with my services. Frightener number one can retire, and they'll bring in the real pro. Frightener number two. And he won't waste time talking to you like this. He'll *tell* you what to do, and my dear you'll be so damned scared you'll do it."

Then she really laughed. She bent forward in such a paroxysm that her negligent cigarette descended on the back of my left hand, and the Rover neatly switched lanes.

"Don't *do* that!" I shouted.

"But you're wonderful," she spluttered. "Didn't anybody tell you?"

"Tell me what?" I demanded. She had no sense of propriety. I eased the car back into the inside lane.

"You *are* number two, Mr Mallin," she said. "They've tried once and failed. Are you the *best* they can do?"

23

I considered that point for a quarter of a mile. The case in question was only a driving offence, which doesn't normally call for frighteners, anyway. Perhaps I was all they'd expected to need. But all the same, there *was* a thousand pounds in that glove compartment.

"Failed?" I said. "What . . . " I glanced at her, " . . . happened to him?"

"The poor fellow's in St Martin's Hospital. I've got friends. Didn't you say that? They dealt with him."

Then I knew why she hadn't been frightened of me. It was about the only thing I did know about the case. The whole thing obviously needed re-thinking.

We were very close to the house by that time, and there seemed no point in prolonging the interview. She'd been leading me on all the while, aware of what I wanted, and aware of how little she had need to fear me. I swept round **into the square.**

"I may have to see you again," I said.

"Do you think you should?" Her eyes were dancing, her lips quivering as though poised for more laughter at my expense. I drew up to the kerb, got out, walked round to her door, and a blow took my left hand off the catch.

I whirled round. "What the hell . . ."

He was taller than I am, wider, uglier, an Indian or Pakistani with lank black hair and a fearsome moustache that drooped with the shame of having to associate with the face.

"My girl, she is," he claimed.

I'd have hit him — I was in the mood for hitting somebody — but then I saw that he was not alone. Six, eight — a whole army of a like type — was slouching behind him, mostly whites, one Chinese, perhaps, but all young and poised, all ready to protect their females.

Toni got out of the car. "Don't be silly, Shri," she said. I thought she'd called him cherie, which would have

25

been quite ridiculous, but I found out later that his name was Shri Ravat.

He growled menacingly. I looked from face to face. A few grinned. One youth carefully placed his guitar on the steps out of harm's way. I recalled the fate of frightener number one, remembered that the beds are hard at St. Martin's, and backed into the car. This was the passenger's side, but I slid across, snapped the locks on both doors, and sat patiently behind the wheel.

Then they began their rocking act. It was unnerving, but not dangerous, and, as you know, I got out of it safely enough.

That was another thing I needed clearing: who was supposed to be frightening whom? I'd need an answer if I was going on with it, and as it seemed that I was frightener number two, I couldn't see any alternative.

After all, if two frighteners fail, there's only one thing left to do.

2

ST MARTIN'S HOSPITAL, quite apart from boasting the hardest beds in the West Midlands, also has the firmest discipline. Did I not realize that this was outside visiting hours, and whom did I wish to see, anyway? Well . . . I didn't know. The only clue I had was that he'd been admitted a week or so before, suffering from . . . something. I didn't want to think what.

"There's the man who has multiple fractures," she offered.

It's a fine, modern reception with a clinically-neat receptionist. A pity it was so cold.

"What's his name?"

"Coe," she said. "George Coe. Are you a friend?"

"Yes," I said stiffly. "A friend."

I remembered Coe. He'd retired a

couple of years before me, suffering from the normal disability of age. Natural wastage, they call it. You can't waste a person like Coe; he's too big, too resilient. He'd been firearms expert at HQ when I knew him, though we'd met only once or twice. I carried a memory of a humourless, plodding bulk of determination.

They'd got him in a private room, no doubt so that his groans wouldn't disturb the rest. He hadn't got any smaller. You know how hospital beds seem to dissolve a patient's size; George Coe made the bed look small. Mind you, they'd put a cage over his legs, and the plaster on his right arm added to the general effect, along with his swollen, battered face.

He looked at me, put down the Ross MacDonald he was reading, and frowned.

"Took you long enough," he grunted.

"I only heard yesterday."

"No grapes, I see."

"I didn't know who it was, so

28

I couldn't judge your taste. What happened?"

He considered me without enthusiasm. I'd been on the case nearly a week, and I didn't know what had happened!

"*They* happened," he said with bitter self-disgust. "I went to the house. Only wanted to see her, and they bounced me."

"Just to see her?"

He shrugged. "Frighten her a bit. You know."

"Hardly your line."

"I need the money."

"It should've been easy. You could pick her up with one hand."

"Then I wouldn't need to," he said savagely. "Just let her see me, I thought. It'd put anybody off."

"But it didn't?" I sat on the side of his bed, and he winced. He'd got a big wince.

"She laughed," he said with hurt dignity.

"Yes, she would."

"Then they bounced me. We were

on the second floor. They bounced me down to the next landing, then down to the hall, then they thought about it and came and bounced me down the steps. Then they jumped on me for a bit."

"It's the herd instinct," I told him. "They've dropped out and reverted to nature. The herd protects its females and its young. She qualifies for both." I looked him up and down. "You were lucky. Serves you right for frightening young women."

"You're not too bright, Mallin," he said. "Got a cigarette? Ta. It was time I was after, to find out what was behind it. You don't hire a frightener just for a hit-and-run. So I needed time to sort something out."

"And the money, you said."

He looked beyond me. His eyes went soft. It was rather disturbing. "I want to get married," he told me. "There's this . . . Anne, her name is. She's got a little house, and I've got a pension, but . . . well, you can't move into her place and take *nothing*. It's

. . . undignified."

It was exactly my own situation. The house was Elsa's; but perhaps I have less dignity. "Yes," I said. "How much money?"

"Five hundred. In cash. An open assignment."

"So at least you're in pocket."

The hand sticking out of the plaster curled up like a knuckled ham. "They came and took it back."

"They?" I said softly.

"There was a solicitor . . ."

"Morrison?"

" . . . who took me on. The same. No mention of a client, but obviously it'd got to be this chap they've got in for the hit-and-run. So maybe he didn't do it, I thought, maybe there's angles. Get a bit of time to work on it, and there'd be five hundred spare . . ." He moved his shoulders in disgust. "So, like a fool, I went to see her. Walked right in. God, I must be getting old."

"And Morrison came for the money?"

He shook his head. "I could've taken

that. A failed contract. But this was two strangers. A big feller, vicious-looking, and a little side-kick you could've swept under the carpet. The money was in the locker. They came and looked, found it, and walked out. And never said a blind word."

I stood up, smoothed his bed-clothes. "No names?"

"The little one coughed."

A clue! I had a clue. The little one coughed. And probably carried a gun as well as germs, because little chaps can't be tough without armament. I looked out at the parked row of decrepit doctors' cars.

"And carried a gun?"

"They both did." He nodded. "It's got a smell, Dave."

"So somebody who can hire armed guns nevertheless pays an old, useless lump of enquiry agent . . . "

"Heh!"

" . . . to frighten a young girl over a hit-and-run offence. Then they up the ante to a thousand . . . "

32

"A thousand!"

"And take on another useless agent to continue the good work. Doesn't that strike you as strange? And why me?" I demanded. "Why come to me?"

He grinned painfully. "Because I recommended you."

I turned from the window. "*You* did?"

"I'd heard you'd set up on your own, and Morrison came to me. So I mentioned you."

"Oh . . . thank you very much. Did he want another loser?"

"Use your head, Dave," he said wearily. "The two goons had been. I knew it had to be something serious. The next thing'd got to be an elimination contract, if the frightening didn't work. So I thought of you. You'd play it cool. Nobody damaged too much . . . "

"Except me."

"You can absorb a lot of damage for a thousand quid."

"And what if I don't want the job?"

"Do you dare to back out?" he asked. "Who'd be next — eh?"

"Maybe," I said angrily, "I'll think of somebody. Lying in one of these other beds, I'll think up another mug to take it on. Who the hell d'you think you are, to recommend me? I don't want your rubbish. It stinks."

"So clean it up," he said soothingly. "Just play it cool."

Cool? I was steaming with anger when I left the hospital, and had to sit quietly in the Porsche for a few minutes before I dared to drive away. But not far. Oh no. I wanted a word with this Morrison character.

He'd come to my office in the first instance, dropping in on me by chance during one of my infrequent visits. He hadn't been vastly forthcoming, but I'd taken the hint. A frightener, that's what he wanted. So I'd taken him on, to save him turning over any more loathsome stones. But I'd looked him up. I would — wouldn't I? He'd got an office in Church Walk, and apparently no partners. Edgar J. Morrison, LL.B, Commissioner for Oaths.

I'd got an oath or two for him.

I parked at the blind end and walked back. The building was old and vaguely ecclesiastical. It lent the area a spurious charm. He might even have been respectable.

A swing door led into a lobby, another into a hall. It was dark. No sound. An arrow I could just see on the wall indicated I should climb the stairs. They were cosily carpeted. A frosted-glass door bore his name in gold and the request to knock and enter. I did. I was in an outer office with a small counter. A bell-push had a printed card against it. 'Ring for attention.' I rang, but nobody attended. So I thumped the counter and shouted, and Morrison appeared, startled, from a side door.

I hadn't decided about Morrison. He was either a most respectable gentleman, or the biggest crook I'd ever met. But the big crooks can't afford to look anything but respectable, and Morrison was a caricaturist's solicitor. Tall and slim, slightly bent from habitual attentiveness, short-sighted from a constant search for legal truth, dry from the dust of eternity's recorded precedents, he approached, now, politely, just a hint of disapproval in his voice, a suggestion of welcome.

"Mr Mallin . . . isn't it?"

"It is. Can I talk to you a minute, sir?"

You see, he'd got me at it. Sir, indeed! But they do that to you with no more than a lifted, bushy eyebrow.

"By all means. Come along in."

Eventually, one assumed, he would fence himself in completely with legal tomes. They stood everywhere in uneasy piles, almost blocked the narrow Gothic window, heaped themselves on his desk, the chairs, the floor. One day he would rise from his work and be unable to find the door, and finally collapse weakly in their dust, to be found years later as a dry old skeleton in, at last, *propria persona*.

I viewed him dimly through a legal screen.

"What can I do for you?" he asked.

"I'm not happy with this thing."

"Happy," he murmured, considering its precise legal definition.

"I'm working in the dark, trying to influence a young woman who doesn't want to be convinced."

He cleared his throat gently. "I didn't anticipate it would be simple. Your predecessor had . . . hmm, difficulties."

"He was beaten up."

"Yes." He looked distressed. "Do, please, try to keep out of trouble, Mr Mallin."

"Oh, I do. I do. But *what* trouble, that's what I want to know?"

"I'm not at liberty to discuss — "

"Oh, come on," I interrupted. "Who *is* your client?"

He moved a volume and peered past it. "You're very inquisitive."

"Cautious."

"Let me just say that it was a car

accident. A woman was knocked down by a car. The young lady — Miss Brent — witnessed it, and has made a statement. She quite simply made a mistake."

"She doesn't think so."

He made a vaguely impatient gesture. "My client maintains that his car was stolen. It was later found abandoned in a dented condition."

"Not dented before it was stolen?"

"Assuredly not."

"Then why," I demanded, "should your client care a damn if it was his car or not — if it was stolen?"

"There is, apparently, a legal technicality involved."

"Apparently!" I burst out. "You're supposed to be his solicitor. You'll be defending him when it comes to court."

"Next Tuesday," he said calmly.

"And there's only an *apparent* technicality!"

He frowned politely at my anger. "The police don't believe it was stolen.

They have gone so far as to charge him. They're holding him in custody — and bail has been opposed."

I moved uneasily. There were still three tomes on my seat.

"Opposed — for a hit-and-run?"

He sat back and considered me as though I was mental. "Didn't I tell you? The charge is murder."

A little light crept through the mist. A murder charge and a client who could hire armed thugs. But the thugs were being kept in the background. Only expendable trash such as George Coe and Dave Mallin were to be exposed to any dangers.

"There's an interesting legal point here," he bumbled on. "My client claims that his car was stolen. He would find it difficult to prove this. The young lady's identification of his car therefore becomes important. The police rely on it as the central building-block of their evidence. If, therefore, she should withdraw that identification, then the stealing or not of my client's car becomes a purely academic point."

"But she's not easily frightened."

"Frightened!" he said, startled. "My dear Mallin, I wouldn't want anyone frightened."

"Persuaded?"

"A better word. But I would prefer that she should simply be made to realize that she's committed an error in observation."

"And if she doesn't?"

"Then we must . . . " He put his fingertips together and rested his lower lip on them. " . . . think again."

"It costs more," I said.

"What does?" One eyebrow was lifted politely.

"This second thought business. You won't find a good eliminator for a thousand quid."

"I don't follow you."

"I think you do. You're telling me that Toni Brent can't be allowed to give her evidence in court."

"But of course she can. As long as it's altered."

40

"So the alternative is . . . " I made a noise with my lips. "Phht!"

"I beg your pardon."

I leered at him. "I get the point. Don't worry, I'll fix it."

"Now really . . . "

"But I'd better see the client."

"I'm surely misunderstanding you!"

"Up the ante a bit," I explained. "He wants a good clean job, he'll have to pay for it." I got to my feet. "I'll see him at the station, then."

Emotion fought its way into his expression. "Mr Mallin, I forbid you to take this attitude. He wouldn't wish to see you."

"Of course not. Keep it anonymous."

"I'll have to contact . . . " He flapped a bit, tried to struggle round his desk and sent a pile of Halsbury flying.

"Contact whom?" I paused at the door. "Who *is* this gentleman who is held for murder?"

"A most respected citizen in the field of licensed clubs."

"Who?" I insisted.

"His name is Camille Petrucchi."

I paused, caught breathless by the fact that anybody could use the name of Petrucchi so lightly, without perhaps dropping his tone with awe, or glancing over his shoulder in fear. But I had to admit that Camille was all right. At least his club was perfectly legal and soberly managed. As far as we'd known when I was in the force, Camille had had no hand in his brother's operations. It was Arturo you had to watch. Arturo had a hand in everything; finger rather, a nasty grubby finger in anything that made money without the stain of legality.

It explained so much. Arturo would not want his brother to be tried for murder. He would not even want his brother in police hands for too long, because Camille, inoffensive as he might be, could have known just a few too many things about Arturo's activities. Oh, it explained a lot of things, such as the two goons who'd visited George Coe. But it didn't explain why the same two goons hadn't been sent to visit Toni in the first place. Her story wouldn't have had to be altered. She wouldn't have had a story to tell any more.

I said: "I certainly must meet your client."

"If you go to the station — " he began.

"Your *real* client, Mr Morrison," I said. "Perhaps you can arrange it."

I could match his calmness any day. I do it by not listening to what I'm saying. This was some other idiot solemnly arranging a meeting with Arturo Petrucchi.

Morrison simply stared at me. Perhaps I was wrong and he was just an innocent tool. But I thought not.

I left him standing in the dust he'd raised, carefully closed his door behind me, and ran softly down his stairs. Murder, I thought. Something was very wrong. As I came into the dark hall I wondered what, and found out as I was twisted round violently and slammed against the wall.

If anyone ever takes you firmly by the wrist and elbow, you can bet it's a policeman. This was two of them, because they had both arms, and if they expected — hoped — I'd resist, they were disappointed.

"You've been to see Morrison," one of them snapped. "Go on, deny it."

"Why should I deny it?" I asked. "I go to see a solicitor — it's not illegal. I work for him."

There was what sounded like a snarl. I turned my head. The one on my left I dimly recognized as Lew Braine. It was the other who'd snarled — or whatever it was supposed to be — a shorter man, but heavy in the neck and jowls.

"By God, Mallin, I'll break your arm if you try to be funny with me."

I looked again at Braine, raising my eyebrows. It took an effort, because in fact the other one *was* very close to breaking my arm.

"Inspector Flagg," said Braine. "This is David Mallin."

"I know who he is," Flagg snapped. "And I know what he's doing."

"Then you know more than I do," I said. "Do you mind letting me go. I don't carry a gun."

As though in disgust at the suggestion that he might be afraid of a gun, Flagg threw my arm away so violently that I nearly pitched on my face.

"You've been trying to get at my witness," he said in disgust. "Deny it."

"You keep asking me to deny things. Why not ask me to admit them?" He moved towards me menacingly and I held up my hand. "Which I don't intend to do. I've been engaged to look into this business, and you must admit it's strange. I mean, you've got him for murder! Damn it all . . ."

I stopped. Flagg was breathing heavily. His head was down, and I'd touched some nerve or other. Braine moved across quickly and put his hand on the inspector's arm.

"Sir!" he said softly.

45

Flagg was growling. "I'll kill him," he whispered, and Braine spoke quietly, quickly.

Then abruptly Flagg turned away. He smashed his way so violently through the outer doors that I thought they'd fall apart, and Braine's final words hung in the quivering air.

" . . . in the car, sir."

Then we were alone. Braine turned to me. He spoke quietly but passionately.

"You bloody fool, why couldn't you keep your mouth shut! The man's near crazy as it is."

"What'd I say?" I demanded.

"You must know."

"Now listen mate, if there's one person who knows nothing around here, it's me."

He was silent. Then a match flared into his face as he lit a cigarette. He flicked the match at me.

"We've been pushing Petrucchi . . ."

"Arturo?"

"Pushing him hard lately. He's into some nasty things."

46

"Always was."

"And now it's drugs. Moving them, we think, not actually trafficking. We don't know. But Flagg's after him, and Arturo's been putting out a few threats. He just let the word get around. You know. But you can imagine the effect that had on Flagg. He just dived in head first and went all out to get something on Arturo. Then this happened. A Petrucchi car . . . "

"Camille's though," I pointed out.

"Camille's yes. But it's still a Petrucchi car. Camille's Cortina — a dark grey model — was found abandoned after the hit-and-run. This woman was killed, and the car had the right dents."

"Clothes fibres?"

"Let me tell it. He's waiting outside. No clothes fibres, no, but the right sort of dents."

"But murder, man! How could it be murder, when he even claims the car was pinched?"

He sighed. "Because otherwise it'd be

too big a coincidence. A Petrucchi car that fits the description Toni Brent gave us as the accident car." He touched my shoulder in emphasis. "And the dead woman was Flagg's wife." He turned to go. "So don't try to influence Flagg's witness, there's a good fellow. He's about ready to smash anything that gets in his way."

I watched him leave, walking out into Church Walk for a better view. He crossed the road lithely to where Flagg was waiting for Braine to take the wheel of the car. Flagg turned to look at me. It was the first time I'd seen his face in full daylight. I wished I hadn't. Such dark venom bridged the width of the street that I felt my arm creak again in sympathy.

I gave it five minutes after the maroon Ford had left the scene, waiting for the tension to leak from my bones. Then I got into the Porsche, lit my pipe, and drove meticulously to my office.

As I've mentioned elsewhere, I rarely called at the office, mainly because the centre of Birmingham is too far from our place in Shropshire if you only sit and wait for no customers. It's not exactly the centre, you understand, off a side street off a side street kind of, in one of those old blocks that're still standing so solidly. I was on the third floor, me being the only one that high in these days when a client expects to be pampered with lifts. As far as I knew there could have been more floors above mine. I'd never checked. It's enough to get up to my place, that last flight narrow and dreary and echoing. And usually so deserted.

This time it wasn't. Half-way up I sensed it, and stopped. The shadows were heavy up there, and seemed even heavier at the very top. The shadow moved and stretched, became of human shape — anthropoid, anyway.

I said, "Good morning," on the off-chance it was a friendly species.

"You're Mallin," said a thin, sharp and precise voice. It was not my day for friendly species.

I climbed cautiously. He had the advantage up there, particularly as he could have been waiting for hours, his eyes by now being adjusted. But he stepped aside, and as I came on to the landing the light I'd blocked on the stairs dimly revealed him. He seemed no larger than me, no broader, no more dangerous, I reached over and snapped on the landing light.

"Ah," he said. "I'd assumed you were still on gas."

The bare forty watt didn't improve matters. At some earlier date a friend had introduced his face to a razor. One half of it had never recovered, being twisted and drawn together grotesquely. As though to compensate, his hair was prettily styled, his clothes perfect, though a little too immature for him, and he'd adopted a prim, emotionless voice which was actually more disturbing than the face. He moved, I saw, with neat precision, beautifully balanced, perfectly poised.

For one second I thought that

Morrison had worked really fast, but the time lapse was too short. He could be Arturo's man, but he'd been waiting quite a while.

"You wanted to see me?" I asked, politely enough.

"Neatly put," he said in approval. "Wanted to see you. Exactly." He walked round me, his hands moving like an impresario appraising a dancer. "You don't look much to me, Mallin. The other was useless. Past your best, too."

"Shall we go inside?"

He reached out a hand. His fingers touched my chin, gently lifted my head.

"Too soft — fragile. What d'you say, Slim?"

I hadn't seen the other one. There was a tentative cough, and then I knew who they were.

"Not inside," said my friend. "Just wanted to take a look at you. You know what you've got to do?"

"I'm getting an idea."

"Well then." he smiled. One half of

his face smiled. One eye brightened. "You do it then — huh?" He flicked dust from my lapels. "And soon."

"You're right, Dainty," said Slim, and the bright eye turned on him. Slim coughed again, nervously.

Then Dainty turned to leave. Slim moved into my field of vision. He was honed down, fine and small, with only his fear holding him together. Part of that fear was of Dainty, part of death. The two were as one to Slim, who hastened now to take the hint that they were leaving. He scuttled for the stairs, unfortunately tripping over Dainty's feet. Dainty grabbed for the stair rail and held himself awkwardly for a second. His face twisted. Slim was very still. Then the moment had passed. Dainty, I saw, prized his nickname, and anything that ruined his poise set free his hatred.

The snarl evaporated. "After you," he whispered.

Slim almost fell down the stairs. Dainty's feet made hardly a sound on the naked, wooden treads.

Carefully I replaced the dust on my lapels and opened up the office. I've got a special lock on that door, supplied by Pinky Fletcher.[1] There's no keyhole, because there's no key, and it opens electronically. All I do is press the top of my fountain pen, which is a miniature transmitter, and the door opens.

I shut it behind me and crossed to my desk, to get what I'd called for in the first place.

In the bottom drawer, which itself has a trick lock and requires a kick in the correct spot, I had a small, tooled-leather case. Encouraged by my special door lock I'd brought the case here, worrying that Elsa might come across it at home. I put it on the desk and opened it. The inside is softly partitioned, with cleaning implements

---

[1] *Sealed With A Loving Kill*

in compartments, a bottle of gun oil, and a neat little Sauer M38 automatic. Pinky Fletcher had got it for me, at a time when *his* ethics were being tested. I picked it out. This gun was a beautiful thing, just the weight for a 7.65 mm, around 6½" long, and it had a double-action safety catch that made it ideal for quick-draw stuff. I snapped out the fully-loaded magazine. I'd never fired the thing in anger, so I emptied the Auto Pistol cartridges into one jacket pocket, in case I should be tempted to do so, and slipped the gun into the other pocket.

This was a presentation case, you understand. To whom do you present such a thing? A retiring MI6 agent? And why'd he need it then? It makes you think.

I was thinking about it as I left the office. The day was right, but there were heavy clouds on the horizon. The car was cold. I drove for home.

The only one frightened around there was me.

3

"**D**AVID!**"** she called as I shut the front door, so I knew I had to abandon the idea of smuggling the jacket upstairs, and of course she noticed the weight when I flung it negligently over a chair. She frowned.

"We're dressing for dinner," she told me, but I'd guessed. She was in her off-the-shoulder magnificence. "Cousin Peregrine's coming."

"Is he staying the night?"

"He's in a hotel in Bridgnorth. No, he's not staying," she said in that comforting tone she used when she knew it was going to be an experience I wouldn't enjoy.

Which would be a change, with Elsa's relatives. The ones I'd met so far had been inoffensive, if ineffectual. But at least it gave me an idea.

"Elsa, you must have dozens of relatives I've never met."

She looked suddenly eager. "Do you want to go visiting, David?"

"Not me. I can't get away. I thought maybe you'd like to."

"On my own?"

I tried to smile. "For a short while." There was silence. It had not met with success. "I'd better go up and change."

"Why should I go on my own?" she demanded.

"I can't be everywhere at once, Elsa."

"Then be here," she said. "With me."

I spread my arms, poised between my jacket and the door. "Elsa, I'm in the middle of something . . . well, awkward. I'd be happier if you weren't available — kind of thing. To anybody."

She stood up, uncoiled it seemed, her full-length dress simply straightening to her full height.

"Don't you think you ought to explain?"

"It's simply that I can't always be watching you."

"You mean there's danger?"

"I don't say that. I'd just feel happier — "

"Happy! Danger . . . to me? What have you become involved with, David?"

"It's nothing you need to know."

"It's something I've got a right to know." She turned suddenly and snatched up my jacket. "And this?" she demanded, before, even, her hand reached the pocket. She slowly drew out the Sauer. "And this, David?" she asked in soft disgust.

"It's not loaded."

"But you're *carrying* it!" she cried.

"As a gesture only. Elsa, I . . . "

Then she threw the gun away from her and it hit the back of the settee with a plop, falling behind the cushion covers she'd been embroidering for the past month.

"Elsa!" I shouted. "I'm doing the best I can."

"And you ask me to run away from my own home . . . "

"That's the front-door bell."

"Doris will answer it. David, we haven't finished discussing this."

I had my hand to the door. "I've got to change."

She threw the jacket towards me. It fell to the floor, and was still there when I got down in my black tie and dinner jacket, Cousin Peregrine being in the dining-room laughing with Elsa over an aperitif. But the gun wasn't. It had gone from behind the cushion covers. I cursed softly, then went to join in the laughter.

Peregrine turned out to justify the warning Elsa had hinted. His only interest was in killing: fish, fowl and fox, not necessarily in that order but as frequently as possible. I murmured noncommittally through the meal, until we retired for coffee and Elsa had to go and freshen up.

"What you after?" said Peregrine, watching me frantically turning the drawing-room upside down.

"My gun." I was eyeing the hi-fi, wondering if she could have hidden it in there.

His eyes brightened. He put down his brandy and helped.

"Is this it?" he said, disillusioned, fishing it from behind the clock on the mantel.

"Much obliged."

"A hand-gun," he said with distaste.

"Yes." I put it in my pocket. "I use it for rats."

"Disgusting. Hadn't ought to allow it."

"What?"

"Gives the blighters an unfair advantage, only one shot to the barrel."

I agreed. "And if they shoot back there's no sport in it at all."

He was still thinking about it when Elsa returned, and from then on the evening progressed without any further hint of animosity. Peregrine declared he'd had a delightful evening as I saw him out.

When I got back, Elsa was standing by the clock.

"You're determined to go on with it, David, aren't you?"

"I don't seem to have any choice."

"You're enjoying it."

"Not exactly."

"If this job of yours is going to come between us — "

"No!" I said violently, and moved towards her. She turned away. "This thing," I said gently, "involves people who might wish to force my hand. They'd strike at whatever I hold most dear. That's why I want you elsewhere."

"Go away?" she asked softly. "Just like that?"

"I'd feel more comfortable."

"And how would *I* feel?"

"I'm sorry. Please, Elsa, there must be somebody . . . Don't tell me. It'd be better if I didn't know."

Her eyes widened. "They might force you . . . "

"I'm playing it safe. Keeping one move ahead."

"You wouldn't know," she whispered. "*I* wouldn't know." Then her voice broke suddenly as she was unable to control the whisper. "Then how would you get me back, David!" she shouted.

Then I watched miserably while she marched past and out of the room; as Elsa watched equally miserably while I marched out of the house the next morning. I'd thought about it all through the night, and couldn't think of any more, or any less, that I could have told her. We hadn't worked out how I might get her back. Maybe we'd think of something later.

So in fact I didn't look back and wave as I drove away, being far too concerned with what I proposed to do, which was to go and have a serious word with Toni. And all the way there I worried about the advisability of it.

It had decided to snow. A parked car gets the stuff built up on the windscreen. I smoked two pipes, stoking my nerve, from time to time prodding the snow away with the wipers. The arc became smaller. I got out of the Porsche while there was still something to see, and ran up the front steps.

I knew two things, that Toni hadn't gone to the college, and that the action began on the second floor. The hall was empty of all but the smell. They apportion the domestic tasks, you know, but they hadn't listed a hall cleaner on the roster. I stood and listened. Faint music descended. No voices. No suggestion that my entry had been noted.

Slowly I climbed the stairs. This building had probably been declared unfit for habitation. The stairs had a visible sag, possibly encouraged by Coe's bouncing, and the banister was loose. I walked close to the wall, but not too close. The layered paper sagged down towards me.

On the first floor landing I paused, and a door suddenly opened. A person came out, a bucket in her hand (the voice was feminine), and shouted back:

"Then empty the sodding thing yourself . . . "

Seeing me, she stopped. The light wasn't good. I think she smiled.

"You're looking for Toni."

"I am."

"Next floor. Third on the right." She nodded. "And you be easy, huh? Play it loose, man, loose."

I decided to play it loose, whatever that was. I'd noted she'd spoken pure English until she'd pulled herself together. I turned to the next flight of stairs, paused when I heard a scream of laughter behind me, then continued.

The stairs had narrowed. The light barely penetrated. There was something slimy on the naked stair treads, and the rail felt greasy. I slowly lifted my head into a smell of curry and concentrated garbage. It was only natural that they'd hesitated longer over their rubbish up there. But they'd hesitated too long.

The music was a guitar. It came from the first room at the head of the stairs, I thought at first from a record player. Then I realized it was live. I had the recording of that Segovia piece by Narcisco Yepes. Narcisco played it better, but possibly the studio had smelt sweeter. I paused, tempted to knock, then the door opened.

He was gaunt and pallid, a ridiculous goatee beard stuck on his immature chin, and carried a guitar of which I caught only a glimpse. But the inlaying was obviously classical, the instrument worth a few hundreds.

"We saw you come in," he said solemnly. Then he giggled. "I'll compose a special mass." He shut the door.

I turned. The third door on the right was open. Ravat stood in the doorway. He beckoned. And I advanced. There were footsteps on the stairs behind me. I looked back. Dimly I saw a face of hair, a malicious grin. A door opened behind Ravat and a Oriental mask peered out. Ravat gestured angrily, and the face went away. There was silence behind me.

"We are having a guest," he said. "Come in, sir, and be welcomed in our excellent quarters."

He stood aside. What could I do but walk in? It was what I'd come for, after all.

The room was large. It could have been a living-room, bedroom, studio. It was not Toni's bedroom, I knew that much from its location, but in the corner there was a mattress with heaped, untidy blankets. The bare, wooden table bore the remains of a few past meals, and the beginnings of a number of Toni's efforts as a sculptress. Or rather, modeller. She was standing at the table in a smock, her hands covered in goo, and was apparently punching a mass of clay into a model of possible significance.

Along a bench against the far wall was the result of Ravat's activities. He did things with iron. What he did was to twist and intertwine them, and project them in sundry directions to produce weird and provocative results. In spite of myself I was fascinated. There was a certain garish beauty about them.

I was a little surprised to see the expensive gas cylinders and the welding torch lying on the bench. I'd thought at first that he mangled this metal with his fingers, tied the wrought iron cold into those improbable shapes. Then I saw the other evidence of means; a gas ring on the end of the bench, an electric fire in the old fireplace, a cupboard stacked with tinned food.

I'd been forgetting that most of these drop-outs were refugees from wealthy families, who would not like to think their offspring were actually starving, and whilst the revolt might initially be against that specific wealth, common-sense dictated that pride should not entirely preclude a hand-out from time to time, if only to perpetuate the revolt. Perhaps they were dropping out only from the painful process of earning it.

"Sell any?" I asked politely.

Ravat said with savage dignity: "Sometimes I donate. The artist is not selling."

"I'm not offering to buy."

Close to, I saw that his bulk was neatly contained, most of it in his shoulders and arms. He'd have looked better with his hair combed and without the moustache, and actually he was quite young. In his early twenties, I supposed. His eyes moved constantly. He was ready to pounce.

"I wanted a word with Toni," I said.

"She is not saying — "

"Let him speak," she said calmly.

His eyes went to her. He made a hissing sound of disgust, then crossed quickly to his bench and took up his torch as though it was a weapon. I moved round so that I could watch him.

"It's about your evidence," I told her.

"I told the truth."

"I'm sure you did. I'd just like to know what the truth is."

"I saw a street accident. This woman — "

"Where?"

"Aston Lane. By the bus stop. I was waiting — "

"For a bus?"

"Yes."

"At what time?"

"Eleven. After. It was the last bus."

"Dark, then?"

"She could see," Ravat cut in sharply.

"She could see," I agreed. "It's well lit?" I asked her.

"Yes. I could see very well. This car drew up — "

"*This* car?"

"Another one," she said impatiently. But I was deliberately pushing her, trying to shake her confidence. "Another car drew up," I said smoothly. "And?"

"She got out. This woman. It was the other side of the road, further along. She waved, and it turned round and went away. Then she started to cross — "

"To the bus stop?"

"I suppose. Then a car came from the other direction." She hesitated. "I'd seen it parked. Seemed to be waiting."

"Yes. Parked. Sidelights?"

"No lights. I'd thought it was empty."

"But you heard the engine start?"

"No."

"But if it was parked?"

"I didn't hear — "

"Ask your questions," Ravat burst in angrily. "Be polite — and then go."

I glanced at him, and in the corner of my vision I was aware that the door to the landing was now open. I turned. They crowded out there, silent in shaggy menace. I turned back to Toni.

"Then the engine could have been ticking over?"

"It could. I don't know." She glanced

nervously at Ravat. "It just seemed to come up fast, then it was past me. The engine was . . . screaming. The woman looked at it. I think she shouted or something, and she jumped, but it picked her up and . . . and threw her against a tree. And the car went away."

"The car. Did you see what . . . "

She turned her head, I think whimpered, and her hand clutched into the pile of clay in front of her.

"Enough!" shouted Ravat. "You leave, please."

It could have been a signal. They came into the room, filtered in with shuffling intensity.

"I haven't finished."

His left hand moved, and a match was alight in his fingers. He tossed the flame at his torch, and it caught it, roaring. He adjusted its cone to hissing blue.

"You will now leave," he decided.

There was a concerted sigh from behind me. I produced the gun. I allowed it to rest on my palm for all to see, switched it round so that the grip was in my fingers, snapped the safety, then walked slowly towards him.

"Put down the torch, Ravat."

His authority hung in the balance. He did not dare to back down, but he couldn't be sure that I wouldn't kill him. His eyes were on mine, brown, with indefinite pupils and discoloured whites. I couldn't read them. Slowly he reached out his left hand for the gun. The flame in his right danced in front of my face.

"You'll not be killing me," he said softly.

Then he took the gun from my hand, gave a gurgle of phlegmy laughter, and put it down on his bench. He bent the flame towards it. He couldn't know that it was unloaded. It could explode in his face. He'd already done enough, but in youthful arrogance he had to carry the bluff to its ignoble end.

He carefully welded the trigger to its guard. Then he picked it up by its wooden grip and placed it back in my hand. I tossed it like a hot potato.

"We have a saying," he said softly. "He who seeks to play the tiger should not wear false teeth."

He was magnificent in victory, standing with a vast grin, the torch still hissing at me with contempt.

I put the gun in my pocket and turned back to Toni.

"What sort of car?"

"A Cortina. Dark grey."

"How do you know it was a Cortina?"

"My brother's got one. I've been in it."

"But there's thousands about. Why *that* one? Why did the police, having heard your description of it, go out and pick that specific car?"

"Heh!" said Ravat. He put his hand on my shoulder.

I whirled on him angrily. "Clever boy! You know about tigers with false teeth. But can *you* protect her from the tigers with real ones? Can you?"

72

"Protect? I protect her from you."

"Don't be a fool. There's some sort of danger here. In Toni's evidence. Let me hear it, then I'll know which way to face."

He drew back his lips, but made no move. I looked again at Toni. "Why that one?"

"It'd got the boot lid open. A few inches. I saw it clearly. And a bit of string holding it down."

I sighed. It had been enough for Ins. Flagg. If the law would let him, he'd hang Camille with that bit of string. I straightened.

"Thank you," I said, with whatever dignity I'd got left. "And now . . . " I looked at Ravat. "Do you allow me to leave peaceably, or do you want to go on and play it alone?"

There was a murmur from those watching him. He switched off the torch. He had a natural dignity. "Make way!" he said, and they did. "He who walks in fear requires room to run."

I didn't actually run, but I was down

those stairs fast, and straight round to Pinky Fletcher, who was nearly in tears over the gun.

"Such a beautiful piece," he murmured.

"With those things," I said, "beauty is in the eye of the holder."

But he couldn't do anything about it there and then. He looked up at me. "Who is it?" he asked.

I knew he didn't mean who'd ruined the gun.

"Arturo Petrucchi."

Without hesitation he opened a drawer, produced a .38 Colt automatic, and slapped it on his bench. "Then you can't go unarmed."

I shook my head. You carry it — you've got to be prepared to use it.

"There's only five rounds, Dave, but you've got to have something."

So I took it, heavy in my pocket, called in at the library to borrow the Register of Electors, had a bite to eat, resisted the temptation to phone Elsa, and went to have a look at the grey

Cortina in the police yard.

Not that I expected to see much. They had a six-foot wall around the station yard, and of course they weren't going to let any old body go grubbing around, so that there was a constable on guard. I drifted past the open gate a few times. The car was more a mid grey than dark, and they had it nose in to the far wall. As Toni had described, the boot was a few inches open, string holding it down, looped several times round the bumper. They'd have had that open, and gone over every inch for prints, but somebody had carefully put the string back. Exhibit No. 1, that was. I'd have liked to see what was holding up the lid inside.

Then I drifted around in the Porsche for a while. The sky was clearing, and wind was whisping at the light, dry snow. Nothing fitted right. I mean — murder by car . . . it's too chancy. Very unprofessional. You can never be sure of killing your victim. But perhaps that hadn't been the intention.

COF6

The Porsche is so distinctive that I was certain I'd be picked up sooner or later. Waiting for it, I headed for Aston Lane, and wasn't surprised when a black Jag-Daimler nosed in after me. I stopped opposite the bus stop, got out, and waited for Dainty to pick his way fastidiously through the snow. Slim leaned against the steering wheel and watched.

"This is where it happened," I said. "You know?"

"Don't be funny, Mallin."

He put a hand on my arm. I lifted his wrist away.

"No need for force."

"He wants a word."

He led the way to the Daimler, opened the rear door, and motioned. I got in. "Let's go," he said to Slim.

And Slim went. He went with a sliding skid of tyres and a burst of slush over Dainty's shoes before Dainty was inside. The car slewed and Dainty scrambled inside, barking his shin on the sill. I hauled him in, my arms round his waist. He dragged the door shut and fell back against the seat.

"Some power in this engine," said Slim with evident pleasure.

Dainty growled. I had his gun in the left-hand pocket of my motoring coat. I could afford to comfort him, and did.

There was no attempt to disguise our route. Perhaps they considered me one of them. I did hope not. We went rapidly across town and on to the outskirts the other side, where the country nudges the last building estate, and where a few solitary houses lie silently down a side lane. The car drifted along it, through almost unbroken snow, to the far end of the lane, where one old house stood alone in a half-acre, bounded at the rear and on the far side by uneven and gorsey common. It was almost hidden in trees.

We turned in to the drive. There was another big black car already parked in front of the house, with a sullen ape waiting behind the wheel. We got out.

The front door opened, and four of us pounded our hard heels across the polished parquet flooring. The hall was quite bare of furnishings. The clatter echoed through the house.

Arturo Petrucchi was in what was intended as a morning-room. A large french window took most of the rear wall. He had a three-seater settee with its back to the window, a deep armchair in the far corner, and four upright kitchen chairs occupied by four upright citizens. Petrucchi was lounging on the settee, his coat on because the room was like a deep freeze.

I wasn't sure what to expect from him. He was known to be schizo or a manic depressive or something. Anyway, unpredictable, and a buffoon into the bargain. He seemed to take a long time getting to his feet, because there was a lot of him. His voice was like a trumpet, that tearing rasp that Richard Strauss liked to use. He came in on the down beat.

"All stand!" he blared. Four goons

did so. "The great Mallin has arrived. Tara!" And he cupped his meaty hand and blew a resounding raspberry.

I always try to meet the mood. I bowed, grinning, and he swept his hand round to catch me across the face with his flying palm, so vigorously that I was sent staggering.

"Now what the hell've you been doing?" he screamed at me.

4

IT'S quite simple, if you want a quiet retreat for a week or two. You locate an empty house for sale, borrow the key from the agent, copy it, and return the original with murmured regrets. These days of stagnant sales — especially in the middle of winter — nobody's going to be around to check for a month or two. So you move in the necessities of life — and there you are.

And there Petrucchi was, a little blurred because he'd jarred my vision; and sitting in the corner, stolidly unimpressed, was a twisted little runt whom I pretended not to notice.

There was obedient laughter around me. Petrucchi grinned as I straightened, brushed myself off, and said, as calmly as I could:

"Been doing what I was paid for."

"Tcha!" He spat at my feet; it wasn't his place. "And what was that? Tell us. Let's hear the good news."

"You ought to know. You did the paying."

"Morrison did the paying."

"But it was you who bought the contract."

Petrucchi looked round the room and spread his palms in abject innocence. "He's been askin' around." He plunged a fist for my lapels, but I stepped back. "Who told you to start askin' around, Mallin?"

"Morrison didn't say not. Said I gotta see the young lady, explain things . . . " I let it die away, looking round at a circle of faces like rocks with lichen clinging here and there. No sympathy. "Ain't I supposed to do some explainin'?" I raised my voice. "He said you didn't like your brother bein' in the nick."

Petrucchi said icily: "He used my name?"

I gave him a leer. "I bin askin'

around." And dodged a back-hander. "Heh! What you mad at me for?"

"Who the hell got me this loon?" Petrucchi bellowed. "Don't he know what's on the ball?"

"I know, I know," I protested.

"Maybe you know too much." Slowly he sat down, made himself comfortable. He considered me. "Or maybe you're too stupid." He looked round. "Heh, he don't look too bright. What d'ya say?"

Nobody ventured an opinion.

"Morrison said no violence," I said persuasively.

"Morrison said! Morrison said!"

"You mean I can?" I was eager, leaning forward.

"They got my brother in there," he shouted. "D'you think I like that! My kid brother. And he never did nothin' at anybody."

"It was his car."

"It was jumped!" he cried in anguish. "Some hopped-up layabout half-inched his car. It was there, behind the club, and in another half-hour he'd've bin on his way to London. Then some crazy bastard nicked it . . . "

"And ran down the inspector's wife?" I asked. I shrugged at his livid expression. "I just bin askin'. But this little bit of a witness, she didn't tell any lies. You know — she tells the truth. So it's gotta be Camille's car."

"Camille!" he shouted. "What's this Camille? Let's have some respect. Mister to you, Mallin."

"Then it's mister's car. You can't get round it."

"So all she's gotta do is go to the nice inspector and say she's made a mistake. You dim or somethin'! She says it was a green Hunter or a yellow Victor. I dunno. Use your head. But she tells him, loud and clear." He waved his arms wildly. "Then it ain't Camille's car any more."

"But she says it is. Loud and clear."

"Then you change it!"

I looked round, as though bemused. He'd spelt it out, and nothing had changed. Then I managed to find a slowly-blooming smile. I tapped my nose with my left forefinger, slid my right hand into my motoring coat pocket.

"You think I'm dim," I said with pride. "But I can take a tip. You don't want her encouraged, you want her *persuaded*."

And I showed him my Colt persuader, lying in my right palm.

Petrucchi bounced to his feet, and just by coincidence the gun turned to face him. I was beaming with pride.

"You're bloody insane," he bellowed.

I cackled. "In front of witnesses, yeh I'm insane. She gets wasted, and everybody swears you said no. Yeah, I get it. It's cute."

"I don't want her dead!" he howled.

"Of course you don't," I said soothingly, watching his eyes go past me in a signal.

I turned, and as Dainty's hand streaked to his empty shoulder holster I pointed the Colt up his left nostril.

"If Dainty's so good with the gun,"

I complained, "why send for me?"

There was a gentle cough behind me. I looked round. Slim was handling a Luger with the caressing ease of a true gunman.

"You want to see Dainty's brains on the ceiling?" I asked.

Slim's eyes brightened. I saw that he did.

"Slim!" Dainty croaked. "Put it away."

"If you say so." Slim sighed. And he put it away.

"Now," I said, "I think we'll go. You boys're too rough for me. No need to make the act too real, y'know. See you around, Arturo."

He said nothing. The air creaked as a roomful of muscle tensed. I nodded to one and all. "Nice to meetcha."

We went out, the Colt now resting behind Dainty's ear. We got in the car.

"You drive," I said. "Then you can come back with the car. Or if you like to play it tough I'll leave you here in the snow, and Slim can fetch it later. You choose."

He chose to drive. I don't think he'd passed his test. Or maybe he was too strung with fury.

"I'll kill you, Mallin."

"No need. I get paid — I do the job."

"You heard what the man said."

"I heard. Take it slow through here, man. You leave it all to me."

He crouched over the wheel. "Touch her," he said savagely. "One hair of her head. Just touch her, and I'll kill you."

"Well now, I didn't think she was your type."

He shook his head backwards and forwards, groaning. "I got to tell you this," he said eventually. "This Brent kid, she's got to change her evidence. Just do that for Petrucchi, and you keep the money. Anything else — *anything*, Mallin — and you're dead."

"No witnesses," I said soothingly. "You don't need to put on an act for me. It's the next on the right."

He tore the car round the corner. Nothing delicate about him now. He sprayed a pedestrian with slush and drew in with screaming tyres behind the Porsche. I got out. I nodded.

"You put the word out, huh? For a good, clean job, send for Mallin."

He drove away savagely. I stood and watched him, waited until the tail-light had disappeared, then slowly breathed out. Sometimes I talk like a fool, hear myself blathering on and can't do a thing to stop it. One day it'll be the death of me. I reckoned I had about two left.

By that time it was dusk. Aston Lane is not busy, being a useful connecting road for the buses, but otherwise residential. It was tree-lined, but none of them quite obscured the street-lights, which were tall concrete columns with swan necks. The lights were blood-red at that time, but it was obvious that a little later they'd flood the street with unshadowed orange light. There was no possibility that Toni Brent could be shaken about that boot lid on the Cortina. She'd *seen* it, seen the string, the boot partly open. And no amount of bribery, coercion or argument was going to change her story.

I got in the Porsche and started the engine. It took me two minutes to find Lake Drive. I drew up in front of a quiet little modern bungalow. He was home, I saw, his car in the drive, and, as Toni had said, it was a Cortina, same model, only this one was white. Her evidence was as solid as a rock.

I walked up the short, straight drive. The lawn was young, the hedge immature. I stood in the small porch and found the bell-push. A light came on beyond the tear-pebbled glass. A young man opened the door.

He would be about twenty-five, and I could see at once that he was Toni's brother. They had the same eyes, some mischief in them, though in his more seriousness, a responsibility. He was a bit bigger than his sister, but not enough to make it impressive.

"Are you Anthony Brent?"

He was in shirt sleeves, relaxing with a glass of stout in his hand. He nodded. "Yes. What is it?"

"You can't know me," I explained. "I'm an enquiry agent involved in the hit-and-run accident your sister witnessed. There was something that I thought you might help me with."

He didn't seem wildly interested in Toni's problems. I found that vaguely worrying.

"What?" he asked.

"I want you," I said, "to help me to kidnap her."

5

A YOUNG girl like Toni, locked in a closed community, would not be wandering around the far outskirts of town at eleven at night, unless on some personal errand. And she'd mentioned a brother, so that it hadn't been difficult to unearth Anthony Brent from the Register of Electors. But I'd been vaguely worried about the fact that she'd been waiting for the last bus. Why hadn't her brother run her back to the house?

It was a thought I'd kept in the background, but now saw was of possibly greater importance than I'd believed.

"You get away from here," he said, waving the glass in agitation. "I don't want anything to do with your lot."

"Our lot?"

"From the house."

That hurt. I said: "Do I look like one of *them*?"

It was a perfectly respectable motoring coat, the hat the curly-brimmed one. He hesitated.

"And would *they*," I asked, "carry a weapon?"

I produced the Colt and showed it to him. He was impressed, so I produced Dainty's snub-nosed Smith and Wesson, and he was even more impressed.

"What the hell!" I thought he'd drop the glass.

"We've got to talk," I said. Then I put the guns away in case he thought they constituted the entire force of my argument. "I believe your sister's in some sort of danger." Which wasn't precisely the truth.

"Christ, with people like you around . . . You mean somebody's going to kidnap her?"

"I am," I said. "But I can't do it alone."

"Oh Lord," he said in despair. "Has

everybody gone crazy?"

But he had not reacted very strongly over the guns, and I realized that he must have become a little immune to the bizarre.

"I suppose it's no good saying you can't come in?" he asked.

"I wouldn't want to put it to the test."

He grimaced and stood back. "But let me take your coat. I'm not having those . . . things brought into my lounge."

I handed it over. It was warm in the house, anyway. Central heating. He took me into one of those through-lounges they're so fond of these days, designed so that you can see the rear garden from the street. There was a decorative stone fireplace in the long wall, but of course no facilities for a fire. The room was untidy, a child's toys everywhere, and I caught a glimpse of a youngster being shooed out of the room before she should become contaminated by the nasty man. I wasn't pleased to see the child, but nevertheless I smiled, looking round.

"Nice place you've got here."

He looked vague, waiting for his wife to return.

"Yes. Toni could be here."

"But she prefers not?"

He shrugged. "Here's my wife — Betty." He looked at me.

"Mallin. I'm pleased to meet you, Mrs Brent."

She was putting on weight and had one of those round faces that should glow with joy of living, but didn't. Her mouth was flexible, variable from tiny for disapproval to big and open for expressing it.

She nodded to me. We were in a disapproving phase.

"It's about your sister-in-law," I told her.

It was as though I'd thrown a switch. "I knew it," she cried. "Didn't I say there'd be trouble? I said that."

"We don't know what it is yet," said Anthony uneasily.

"But we can guess." She clenched

93

her teeth decisively on the words. "Ever since she got in with those horrible flower people, I knew there'd be trouble."

"I don't know that they're actually the flower lot," I said, "and this hasn't got anything to do with them. When she left your house that night and went for the bus . . . " I glanced at Anthony, who looked away. " . . . she witnessed a car accident. It's her evidence that's the trouble."

"There!" cried Betty. "If she hadn't been going back to that terrible house . . . "

"You could say that," I agreed equably. "And of course if she hadn't got in with that crowd, and if she'd been properly absorbed into a normal society, she might have been more prepared to lie about the whole thing, if only for a bit of peace and quiet."

They stared at me. There was nothing but antagonism from the wife, but Anthony was caught in an agony of indecision, weighing his loyalties. You could see what had happened here. Toni had visited, perhaps to wish them a Happy New Year — bowing to convention — and had met with her sister-in-law's opposition. Maybe Toni had been testing the mood, feeling perhaps a certain boredom with her friends at the house. But how could she be so disloyal as to join in a condemnation of them? The evening would have ended painfully, with Anthony tormented over his responsibility for his younger sister, and conceding to his wife so far as to allow Toni to take the last bus home.

"I've been employed to persuade her to tell a lie," I explained. "She refuses." Anthony nodded. That much he could understand. "But it's very important to somebody for her to tell that lie, and very soon it will become imperative that she should. Am I being clear? The pressure on Toni will become greater, even unpleasant. She will just not be allowed to give her evidence, as it stands."

"No!" cried Betty. "You're not going to involve us."

Anthony didn't glance at her. His eyes were on me, that same unflinching gaze that I remembered in Toni. He said:

"As it stands? Could she have made a mistake?"

"She made no mistake," I told him. "Her story stands up from all angles. So — if she tells a different one in court, it'll have to be perjury."

He snorted, turned away, and punched a cushion.

"I'm not having it," said Betty firmly. "She's been nothing but trouble, and she's not bringing it into *my* house. Not if I've got any say in it. She made her bed, let her go and lie in it."

I sat down on their studio couch and filled my pipe, whilst she unearthed her store of platitudes. I was not overly worried by her outburst of venom. It was based on fear — for her social standing, her security. I waited.

She rounded it off. "And if she

thinks she can bring her troubles into this house, she's mistaken. We've got no cause to worry what happens to her. I don't feel sorry for her. No, not one little bit."

I puffed smoke at their branched ceiling fitting.

"It's not your feelings that're in question, Mrs Brent. As I said, there's going to be pressure put on Toni, and the classic method is to strike at a person's emotions. You've got a nice place here. And every item in it, including yourselves, is completely vulnerable. The threat will not come to Toni's health — or her life — but to yours and your child's. And if that happens, can you be so sure she'll agree to change her story? Or is she going to say: 'I've got no cause to worry what happens to them.'? Ask yourself that."

She asked herself. "She's unreliable, thoughtless, selfish . . ." And she stopped, appalled by what she had said.

"Exactly my impression," I agreed, smiling from one to the other. "Can we allow such a person to run around loose?"

"You've got to see her, Anthony," she cried. "Talk some sense into her."

"Oh — do be quiet," he said in exasperation, and she looked at him as though he'd struck her. He turned back to me. "Cutting out the fine words, how does it leave us?"

"If she's not available, to anybody, nobody can challenge her loyalty. Or do you want to put it to the test?"

He dragged his fingers through his hair. "You and your arguments! You're not logical. Even if she's not available — as you put it — they can still . . . take action against my family. They'd assume she'd hear about it, wherever she was."

"Not if they believe her to be dead."

Betty gasped, and Anthony made a sharp gesture. "Why should they believe that?"

"I've gone to some trouble to lay it

on. If she now disappears, that'll be the assumption."

"And why should I trust you?"

"Everything depends on your trust. Without it, there's nothing I can do."

"And what do you intend?"

"That you should go to the house and bring her out. There's no one else she'd leave with, or who could get to her safely. Then you bring her to me."

"My God, you're asking a lot."

"I am. But some day you've got to make your own decisions."

"Go to the house!" Betty cried. "To that place?"

"I could live through it," he said.

"But you're not going to?" she asked.

"I'm thinking about it."

I stood up. "It's all I wanted. You think about it. I'll be waiting in Water Lane at about ten tomorrow morning. I'll have a red Dolomite Sprint."

"And you'll take her away?"

"I'll take her away."

"Which would be just what you'd

want," he said, "if you really intended to kill her."

I grinned at him. "Makes it difficult, doesn't it? Can I have my coat now?"

He went and fetched it, hefting its weight doubtfully. I nodded good night to Betty, and Anthony saw me out to the porch.

"That's not a Dolomite," he said.

"No. It's too distinctive, though."

"It's nice to have a choice," he said wistfully. And I knew he wasn't talking about cars.

I watched him go inside. The air was crisp and dry. There was no car in sight, and if I'd been observed it would be sheer bad luck. There was a chance it would work.

Then because I was on the right side of town, I drove home.

My headlights shone on the Dolomite in the garage, but no Rover. I ran inside the house. Doris was in the kitchen.

"Where's Elsa?"

"She's gone."

"Gone where?"

She was making pastry and did not look up. "I don't know. She took a few cases."

"But she didn't say where?"

"She doesn't confide in me."

Oh, but she did. She confided everything to Doris.

"Maybe," I suggested, "she told you I wasn't to know."

She sniffed. "She told me *I* wasn't to know."

"I hope that's true, Doris."

Then she looked directly at me. "Are you calling me a liar, Mr Mallin?"

"Doris, I asked Elsa to go away. I asked her not to say where. But she'd perhaps tell you, and there're people who might want to find out. I wouldn't want to think they could find out from you."

Her eyes were brittle. "Just let them try."

"They may."

She looked at me scornfully. "I wouldn't have any truck with such people, sir, even if they might be your friends."

There was no message left for me, which was unlike Elsa, no note anywhere saying how we might contact each other. I hoped she realized that she did not dare to phone either the house or my office. Not after tomorrow, anyway.

It was a miserable evening. Doris turned up her usual perfect meal, and it was tasteless. Why should I have been so restless? It was what I'd asked Elsa to do, after all. But I couldn't settle to the tele, even failed to be soothed by an LP of Mozart on the hi-fi. By that time we'd got the lot — transcription turntable to bass reflex speakers, a stereo tuner and a cassette deck — and I was not interested in any of it.

Elsa had left no message.

Also, I realized, she'd removed all chance of my backing out of the case and giving back the money to Petrucchi. I'd left the thousand quid in the Rover's glove compartment.

Fortunately, she hadn't taken the keys to the Dolomite, or things might have gone wrong. But ten o'clock the next morning found me parked quietly in Water Lane. I was still waiting at ten-thirty.

Then at last they appeared, Anthony with his hand firmly on his sister's arm. It hadn't been an easy job for him; he was distinctly ruffled. And Toni was still making trouble, protesting and gesticulating. She was wearing a flowing, fringed garment down to her ankles, and a lot of beads. Anthony came to a halt beside the car, and I got out.

"Oh no!" she said, drawing back. "Haven't you done enough talking?"

"It's gone beyond talk," I said. "Will you get into the car?"

She tried to tear herself away from Anthony. He hung on grimly, his face tight and pale.

"It's all right, Sis. All right."

"Oh no it's not," she protested.

103

"Don't you know what he is? And he carries a gun."

"Not at the moment," I said. "And I'm not going to touch you, or in any way force you. All I want you to do is to trust your brother."

"He's coming with us?"

"No. It's better he shouldn't know."

"Then I refuse."

"Now Sis . . . "

"No," I said. "Take your hand off her. Let her walk away if she likes. Toni, I want to take you somewhere where you'll be safe, and where it'll make it safe for your brother's family. But it's got to be now. No 'ifs' and 'buts'. We've got a chance of getting clear, but it may not come again."

"I can't just . . . go."

"But you can, and you must."

She looked at Anthony. He smiled, shrugged. "It's all right."

Then she got in the car, as simply as that, something having passed between them.

I left him standing forlornly on the

pavement, his eyes shadowed with doubt, and then I drove. I had to be absolutely certain I was not being followed, and it necessitated pushing the Dolomite to the limit, way out into open country, before making a big sweep back towards Birmingham.

Toni sat quietly, her hands in her lap. I glanced at her.

"I suppose you realize I haven't had any breakfast," she said severely.

"Good for you. An empty stomach sharpens the brain."

"There's nothing to think about."

"Oh yes there is. You may not realize it, but you're a very important young woman. Your evidence about the hit-and-run is absolutely vital. So I'm going to hide you away. You'll be free to leave whenever you like, but if you do it'll waste a rather grand effort by your brother, and it'll cut the ground right from beneath my feet."

"I don't know that I'm worried about the ground under your feet. Unless you need it for running on."

"I need a bit of time," I told her. "I want to arrange things so that you become less important to everybody. It's your evidence that the police are relying on, so I hope to be able to prove their case without it. Then you won't matter any more. You'll like that."

She grimaced at me, and looked round as we drew to a halt at the kerb.

"This it?"

I nodded. It did, in fact, look like a prison, one of those unfortunate buildings that was conceived without grace or imagination in the early part of the century, five storeys of red brick and small windows, everything geometric, everything solid, and all surmounted by little turrets and peaked gables. Now it was a block of flats. I took Toni inside, and we climbed. Each landing was alike; all the corridors matched. Faint sounds of occupation came from the various flats, but everybody kept to himself, and nobody cared about us. At the very top, I paused.

"This is all one flat up here," I

explained. "The owner's. You'll like her."

You had to like Ruby Streiss, or you just turned and ran. She swung open the door . . . "Well, David!" . . . swept us inside, flowed over us and round us with a volatile enthusiasm that could either drown you or wash you up on her glorious shores, and fussed over Toni. "Why, you beautiful creature. David, she's splendid. Where did you find her?"

Ruby was wearing huge, flaring slacks that started vast around her middle and finished up like a tent above her sandals, and a sequined blouse that she either hadn't troubled to fasten or could no longer do so. Her magnificent breasts swung in and out of the sparkling screen, unconfined by anything plebeian such as a bra. She bounded round us as though we'd come for sacrifice and she was planning the ceremony.

This was Ruby's studio, a whole half-floor of it, with north-facing windows and all the encumbrances of her various arts — or crafts. Ruby had no pretensions towards being artistic. She had no desire to explore her soul, only an uncanny knack of feeling out the market. She did everything; painted in any medium, sculpted, ceramiced, appliquéd, and all with a naïve and touching belief that she had no special ability.

Ruby was in this country on forged papers. She didn't know that I knew. Pinky Fletcher didn't know that I knew he'd forged them for her. I think he was in love with her, but of course nobody could marry Ruby Streiss. She'd be just too much to take on. Besides, I reckon she was nudging sixty.

"This is Toni," I said. "She models."

"And quite right, too. Such a splendid figure shouldn't go unrecorded."

"In the other sense," I said. "She models in clay."

"Nonsense."

"And she's come to stay for a few days," I finished.

"Then she *will* model," Ruby said in delight. "For me. I'll capture her on canvas and in marble."

And strangely Toni blushed. I grinned at her. "She hasn't brought a thing with her."

"What does she need?" Ruby demanded. "Come here, child, let's see you in the light. Isn't it splendid? This wonderful snow. The light's so pure and clean. You must have white light, you know. Must have it."

As there seemed every likelihood that she'd have Toni down to the buff in a couple of minutes, I thought I'd break in.

"Ruby, I told her she can leave any time that she likes."

"Leave!" Ruby glared at me. Her glare is like the sun rising. "Why should she want to go?" She turned back to Toni. "What's this about modelling in clay?" she demanded. "It's got no colour, my dear. Can't waste the light, can we? I'll get you doing oils. Oh yes." Then she had a vast and overwhelming idea. "You can paint *me* in the nude."

"Oh no," said Toni faintly.

"I insist." She roared with laughter. "Lady Trying to Get Into Bath — after Degas. It'll slay them at the Academy."

I grinned at Toni, winked, and quietly left.

Nobody was watching the Dolomite. I got away smartly and headed for my office, just in case anyone had seen me leaving home and wondered where I'd been heading.

Maybe they had, or maybe they were just waiting. The maroon Cortina that I recognized as Flagg's was parked outside the office block. I could have driven on, trusting to the change of car to disguise me. But I had to face it some time. I drew up, climbed out casually, and Sgt Braine got out from behind the Cortina's wheel. He came over, looking strained.

"The inspector wants a word."

Strange that they all used the same phrase. "Where is he?"

"In his car."

So Braine had been driving only to allow Flagg to sit in the back, giving me room to slide in beside him.

Ins. Flagg seemed sunk down between his own shoulders. I got the impression that he was deliberately forcing himself inwards, containing himself against any outbreak that might undermine his grasp of the situation. His eyes were bleary from lack of sleep, his hands locked on each other in some sort of entwined mystery. No doubt it would take some time to free them, long enough for him to hold back a blow.

He stared straight ahead. "The young lady — Toni Brent — left the house this morning with a man. She has not been seen since."

"It's only lunchtime. Early days."

His voice continued in a croaking monotone. "She did not go to the art college, it's been too long for shopping. So where could she be?"

"It's one of life's little mysteries. It wasn't me she was with."

The eyes turned and held me. His

voice hardened. "I'm aware of that. The man was slighter, younger, more gentlemanly."

He intended this in no way as an insult, simply an observation.

"And you're asking me for ideas?" I asked.

"I'm putting two and two together, Mallin. I'm seeing that you had an interest in her, and I believe you were supposed to be frightening her into changing her evidence."

I smiled at Braine, who was twisted round in the front seat. It bounced off. "I didn't notice she was frightened."

"Maybe she was more frightened than you think," Flagg grated. "You're not an inspiring sight, Mallin." His voice dropped an octave. "And take that smirk off your face before I knock it off." His fingers writhed. I looked away from them.

"Perhaps she's run away," I suggested. "If she can't stand my ugly mug."

"But I want her, Mallin. I want her where I can see her. You understand?

So — produce her."

"I don't know where she is."

"Liar!"

"I don't want to frighten anybody," I said. "It's me who's frightened."

He said nothing, searching for signs of fear in my eyes.

"Sarturo's in town," I explained.

I'd known what it meant as soon as I'd seen the twisted little figure of Emilio Sarturo crouching in the corner of Petrucchi's room. There had been mention of drugs, of Petrucchi moving them. Now there was no doubt. Sarturo was the biggest supplier in London, and if Petrucchi was working for him there was trouble ahead. But why should Sarturo care about Camille and a hit-and-run charge?

Flagg went very still. The fingers were locked into one powerful, distorted mass.

"Sarturo," he whispered. "Where?"

"I'd rather stay alive."

"With Petrucchi?"

"In Arturo's house."

"Then you've been there?"

"Forcibly invited."

"And now my witness has disappeared."

"Coincidence."

"What did you speak about?" he demanded.

"Arturo seemed concerned that some harm might come to Toni Brent. He forbade me to touch her."

"Mallin!" he said dangerously.

"So of course I haven't."

"Get him out of here," he growled. Braine stirred. "Get him out of my car," Flagg roared, and the hands fought to free themselves.

I got out, without Braine's help, and watched them drive away. Flagg shouldn't have been on this case; it was too personal. He was too close to a breakdown for my liking. I needed people around me whose actions I could trust, and Flagg was beyond any reasonable predictability.

I trotted up to my office, or rather I trotted up the first flight and panted the rest. Too much smoking. I'd only gone up to use the phone, and Doris said she'd heard nothing from Elsa.

"Shall you be home for dinner?" she asked.

"No." She meant the evening meal. "Expect me when I arrive."

Then I went for a bite and wondered how long it would be before the storm broke around me, deciding to find out as much as I could before it did.

Camille's place was just outside town, and had probably been a wayside café at one time. But he'd tarted it up, raised the standard of the meals, and he'd finished up with something very tasteful and profitable. No gaming, you understand. A little dancing, the occasional cabaret of second-rate talent, every now and then a startling combo on its way to the stars. He called it the Carimba, and if you were dressed right and had the correct face you could possibly get a table.

I wasn't dressed right, but I didn't want a table, and anyway it was too early. The neon signs were cold and dusty, but a soft light glowed somewhere behind the foyer, and there was exploratory music dimly on the cold night air. I was not interested in the front. The back for me.

I walked right through the customers' car park on my way round. There'd have been room for a hundred cars there, and probably it had been packed on the night of the accident. So imagine somebody intending to run down the inspector's wife. That somebody would have to be a person involved with or employed by Arturo Petrucchi, with instructions to go out and kill. It was reasonable to suppose that Arturo could have been at the club that night, along with one or two of his cretinous retinue. But would the selected goon be so stupid as to take Camille's car to do it with? Could he not have found one other car left unlocked in the public car park, and used that? Or even stolen a car from somewhere else. Why Camille's? And why Camille's with something in the boot, making it recognizable?

I wandered round to Camille's private bit. There was no difficulty in entering it, or in driving from it, but it was sufficiently private to justify Camille having left his keys in the car.

Or key? Singular. Ah yes, that was a thought. If he'd left only one key in, that raised entirely different ideas.

This was the rear entrance to the club, part of the area being taken up by empty crates and kegs. Four steps led down from the swing door, and a small window beside it was lit. I stood and imagined the car, standing there that night, and the door behind me swung shut with a thunk. I turned.

Dainty was standing on the top step. He wore a shortie coat over an immaculate dark suit, and driving gloves. He might presumably just have driven in at the front.

"Key," I said. "Camille claims he left his key in. One, was it, or a bunch?"

"One key." Dainty delicately trod down the steps. "It's all it needs, the same key for ignition, door and boot. The duplicate was in the office safe."

"Makes it interesting, doesn't it?"

"To you, perhaps." He looked vaguely round the small area. "Mallin, the Brent girl has gone missing." He slowly returned his gaze to my face.

"So I've heard."

"But you didn't hear what Petrucchi said. No killing. He said that. If he'd wanted that, he'd have asked me to do it. But he paid you, Mallin." His voice went slick as ice. "What have you done to her?"

It suited me that Petrucchi should believe Toni to be dead. Then he wouldn't search for her. I brought out my most stupid leer, and produced one of those exaggerated Jewish shrugs, shoulders high, palms up and out.

The Jews must be a peaceable lot to have developed such a gesture. It leaves you completely open to attack. Dainty slid in smoothly, each foot

118

perfectly placed, and sunk his right fist to the watchstrap in my stomach. I was completely unprepared, no time to flex muscles, and the pain tore into my guts, the breath fought to discover a way beyond the agony. I rolled ingloriously at his feet.

He smiled down at me. This was Dainty without Slim, and with no need to maintain an image. It was pure and unadulterated Dainty, efficiently vicious and coldly controlled.

"Oh no," he said softly. "You haven't killed her. Not you. You're too soft. Don't you think I know what it takes, Mallin? And you haven't got it."

"Perhaps," I managed to gasp, "she's run away."

"Now that would be unfortunate. Because it means you'll have to find her. And you'll have to find her damn fast, because there's got to be time to persuade her."

I began to struggle to my feet. He reached out a hand to help me up. I should have been suspicious that it was his left. He yanked me towards him, then he smashed me back with his right fist in my face.

"And if *you* can't persuade her," he said, "then somebody else will have to try."

He moved me with his foot. "D'you think you'll be able to drive?" he asked kindly.

"I can drive."

"Then I suggest you drive to wherever you've hidden her, and produce her."

Then he calmly mounted the steps and thrust the swing doors open. Its closing thump seemed to be the final blow to my self-esteem.

Oh yes, I could drive. I could just about get in the car and fumble it along the road to home. But there was no Elsa, no warmth or encouragement, only Doris to stare at me with pursed disapproval, and a cold, merciless bed.

6

AND of course, when I wanted him there was no sign of Lew Braine. Any other time he'd keep popping up all over the place, but the next morning there just seemed to be nobody appraising my movements. There was a car following me, of course, but it was an ordinary patrol car, so it wouldn't be him.

I waved the car down and asked them, but they didn't seem keen on locating him on their radio. "He's gotta eat, mate," said one them, which gave me an idea.

Police stations are designed like theatres, all impressive drama and bright lights at the front, and a drab rear entrance for the workers, which the public never sees. It so happened I'd been inside this one, and vaguely remembered its layout.

The rear entrance was from the yard. With that amount of knowledge to start with, it only takes a bit of confidence.

He was still patrolling the yard, but if you drive in casually, give him a salute, grin at him, park, and walk directly towards the door, it takes him so long to decide whether you're visiting brass that you're inside before he can move.

From then on, you play it as it comes, working from years of experience of what to expect.

The CID room, I'd noticed when I parked, overlooked the yard, and I had no desire to get involved there, so as there was a corridor heading directly away from me I strolled ahead. A loud voice rang from a room on my right. Keep going, Mallin. And then the corridor branched, and from the left was the smell I'd been sniffing out. The Police Canteen. Braine had to eat sometime. Come to that, so had Mallin.

A door almost in front of me

crashed open. Inspector Flagg's voice rang out. "I don't care how many men it takes. Find her." A uniformed sergeant backed out and closed the door tenderly behind him. He straightened and looked at me.

"Keep clear, mate," he said. "The old man's flying high."

So I headed for the canteen.

Police canteens are much the same as others, except that the tea urn has a tendency to be larger, and the ladies behind the counter work flat out because coppers eat all the time.

I joined a small queue, seized a tray, and looked casually round. Braine was sitting at a small table in the far corner, and alone because he was obviously too moody to approach. I got my stuffed heart and bread pudding and approached him.

"May I?"

He moved his empty cup and his polished plate to make room, and glanced up.

"Mallin! You damned fool."

"I had to talk to you."

"What's happened to your face?"

"Somebody likes me even less than you do."

He grunted. It seemed unlikely. "You know Flagg's looking for you?"

I dived into the stuffed heart. "I know he's looking for the girl."

"But you couldn't help him with that?"

I shook my head. "Why is he still in charge of the case? The man's obviously nearly out of his mind."

"You don't know him." Braine lit a cigarette. He bent forward over the table confidingly, but there was a possibility he only wanted to make a quick grab if I made a break for it. "You don't know how much he adored his wife. He stuck her up on some sort of idealistic pedestal, and couldn't ever do enough for her."

"Possessive."

"No." He said it a little too violently. "No," he said again. "You should have seen him that night. Of course, we all knew about the threats that'd been floating round, but we'd all assumed they were aimed at Flagg personally. He loved that. It made it an all-out fight. He was going to get Arturo Petrucchi, and it was only a matter of time. And then that thing happened. It was . . . " He stubbed out the cigarette. " . . . shocking. We were all appalled. Flagg was off duty that evening, and the thing landed in my lap. At first it was just a hit-and-run. You know. So I sent out a message for him, and we got on with it."

"With questioning Toni Brent?"

"Of course."

"And you accepted every word she said?"

His fingers tapped impatiently on the table. "Why not? There was no reason she'd lie, or make a mistake."

I was polishing my plate, as he had, with a piece of bread. "I happen to know she was emotionally disturbed that night."

"Oh come on, Mallin. That's just a

try-on. There was no sign of it when I questioned her."

"Not upset?"

"About the accident, of course. She'd seen a woman killed. We'd about got to that when I noticed the inspector had come in. He was so *quiet*, Mallin. Lord, I feel cold every time I think of how quiet he was. Just nodded for me to get on with it, and listened, and his eyes were strange. So I got on with it, and you know, Mallin, you won't accept this, but he's really left it to me ever since."

"It's not the impression I got."

"He *knows*, you see. He's a strange man. Behind all that fury and shouting, he's ice cold. He knows he can't operate normally, but he's here in the middle of it, and we both know I'm running it."

I looked away from Lew Braine's eyes. There was something deep down inside them that I didn't like and couldn't interpret. Was this some sort of hero-worship, or did Braine hate his inspector, and was simply carrying him on to a victory that would be the sergeant's, and perhaps could be Flagg's swan-song?

"So you're running it," I conceded. "Congratulations. And at what point did you know it was Camille's car that had killed her?"

"When we found it. That was hours later, dumped down a cul-de-sac in a housing estate. Flagg'd gone home — "

"But you'd know every car run by the Petruccis. And there'd been threats. Didn't you link it up straightaway?"

"We were treating it as an accident, at first."

"And Flagg didn't realize his wife had been murdered?"

"I went to his place to tell him."

"And it hasn't occurred to any of you that the thing's all crazy? The car, Lew, the car. If they'd wanted to kill Flagg's wife, it's the last car they'd use."

"True . . . true."

"And if they'd got something big going — and the presence of Emilio Sarturo seems to confirm that — the last thing they'd want would be to raise the wind."

"A blind," he suggested blandly. "A diversion."

"Rubbish. And there was something in the boot, holding it open."

"A beer keg," he said. "On end. An empty beer keg."

"Good Lord. So why would Petrucchi or any of his mob put a beer keg in the back, on end, in order to go out and kill Flagg's wife?"

He smiled vaguely. "We may find out."

"And the key?"

"Camille had left it in the ignition."

"The duplicate being in the safe?"

"As Camille claimed."

"Then don't you realize," I burst out, "that whoever did it — "

"If it was not Camille," he said quietly.

"Would have had only one key to do two jobs."

"Your pudding's getting cold."

I attacked the bread pudding

vigorously. "The boot of a Cortina hasn't got a handle," I explained. "So if you want to tie it down, pretty-well all you can do is put the key in the boot lock, and hook string over that. There's just nothing else to tie on to. So, that disposes of the key Camille left in. Lew, it means that whoever took the car would've had to short-out the ignition in order to drive it. Was it shorted-out when you found it?"

"It wasn't."

"Then he removed the wire before he left it."

Braine didn't say anything for a moment, moved the cup and saucer around slowly with his forefinger, and looked up at me.

"You love it, don't you! This theorizing. Well, you've got it wrong. The key in the boot lock wasn't Camille's ignition key, it was another one, a key entirely foreign to the car. Wedged in. No, Mallin, whoever it was who drove that car simply used the key that Camille had left."

129

He was being very informative. I wondered why. His eyes were watching me carefully, as though he waited for what I might suggest.

"A key in the boot lock belonging to another car?" I asked.

"Yes."

"But Camille doesn't own another car." He was beginning to irritate me — perhaps intentionally — so compliant, so calm.

He smiled, a gentle reflex of the lips. "But of course, you're working for Camille. You're very persuasive. Mallin."

"I'm trying to be logical."

"Be too logical," he murmured, "and it makes no sense at all."

I couldn't accept that I'd interpreted his tone correctly, and waited while I worked on it. The same answer kept coming back.

"You believe that?"

"I wait," he said. "Watch and wait."

"You don't believe you've got a case against Camille, do you?"

"I'll get some more tea."

I clamped my hand over his wrist. "What's going on, Lew?"

He sat down again. "He wants Arturo Petrucchi," he said softly. "Not just because of his wife, but for a year — two years — he's wanted him. It's become an obsession. And now he's got Camille. It may not be much of a case, but he's going to push it until Arturo does something. Sometime, Arturo will *have* to act. And then we'll have him. We'll tie him down . . . "

"And meantime?"

"We push and we push, building up the pressure. Because now the inspector's wife's dead, and if he pushes a little beyond reason, no one will care. They'll understand."

"They ought to take him off it."

"Oh no." He shook his head. One lock of that blond hair drifted over his eyes. "Because here we can watch him. Send him home, and he'll break out where we can't control it. But here?" He brought his palms together with a quiet little slap. "Here we can *use* his violence. Excuse it. Let it ride way beyond what is reasonable. And who knows, a little of that rage of his might leak through to Petrucchi. And nudge him, Mallin. Nudge him into that one mistake."

No, it wasn't like any other canteen. The clatter was the same in the background, but there in the corner was an eddy in the activity. The current lapped against something washed in from the sanity out there. It moved, and I didn't want to see.

Lew Braine was telling me. He was saying that Flagg was possessed by a boiling rage and a terrifying determination. Yet behind it all there was an icy-cold decision to use that rage. It was *his* decision, Flagg's, not the sergeant's. Braine was going along with it, but the purpose was Flagg's. That a man could coldly use his own agony and distress I found so appalling that I could say nothing.

"So you see, Mallin," he said, "why

you must bring the young lady back to him. Everything rests on her evidence. The fact that it's there, she's there — you understand?"

"No doubt she'll turn up in time for the hearing."

"And you expect me to accept that?"

"She's a free agent. If she's hiding away, she'll have good reason."

"I'm concerned about you, Mallin."

I pushed back my chair and stood up. He made no attempt to detain me.

"Perhaps you'd better worry about yourself, Lew," I told him. "This inspector of yours is too subtle for my liking. You say he's letting you run it. Perhaps he wants you around when the thing blows wide open. Think about it."

He twisted his lips in bitter humour. "Do you think I haven't? But I owe him."

"Perhaps he realizes that." And I was pleased to see that at last I'd caused his eyes to flicker.

I walked out of there, my legs strangely stiff, so involved with what he'd said that I walked right out into the main corridor without sensing for the possibilities.

From the front part of the building two plainclothes men were leading a third man towards Flagg's office. I paused, but it was too late. Anthony Brent's head came up, and he couldn't suppress the recognition. But he managed to convey a sense of reassurance before they took him in to see Flagg.

I was not confident that he could oppose the inspector. I turned towards the rear, and saw that Lew Braine was watching me from the door of the canteen.

Out, I thought. Out of that yard as quickly as possible, but before I'd got the car door properly shut, Braine was leaning on the roof.

"That was her brother," he said.

"I know." There was no point in denying that I did. Anthony would have to admit something, at least that he'd met me.

"He fits the description of the man who visited her."

"Not unlikely. A brother may visit a sister."

"But since then she's disappeared."

"Then perhaps," I said, "he's hidden her away in some quiet little hotel. I did suggest that."

"You did? When?"

"I went to see him the other evening. I was trying to find a hole in his sister's evidence."

"But you didn't?"

"I found they'd had a row. I told you, she was emotionally upset."

He slapped the top of the car. "Oh, you're quick. Congratulations, Mallin. I do hope we meet again."

I nodded, backed out, and drove from the yard. The constable saluted. Nice chap.

Then, as there seemed to be nothing more to discover about the killing, I went home.

I was early. But not early enough. I'd missed them by half an hour.

Doris opened the door. I'd never seen Doris ruffled, and even then there was only an atmosphere to go on. Perhaps she shut the door after me too sharply.

"Sir," she said, "two gentlemen have called, while you were out."

"Gentlemen?"

"Rough persons."

"And what happened?"

"I sent them packing," she said with pride, but though her head was high, she was lying. I knew.

Doris was badly frightened.

7

"SIT down, Doris," I said.

"Sir?"

I wished she wouldn't do that. Elsa's always been Elsa to her, but for me it was always sir or Mr Mallin. I sat her down and went to get her some brandy.

We were in the drawing-room, and no doubt when Elsa and I were both out she'd be sprawled all over the furniture with her feet up. But now she was prim and upright.

"The two men," I said. "One little chap and one with a scarred face?"

"No. They were both big." She gulped the brandy. "Both ugly."

So probably Petrucchi's. "And did they hurt you?"

"Only my arm."

"I'm sorry. Why didn't you phone the police?"

She tossed me a wicked little glance. "I thought they *were* the police. Sir." She recovers fast, does Doris.

"What did they do?"

"One of them went through the house, top to bottom, while the other one watched me."

"Did they say anything?"

"They asked me where Elsa had gone."

"Which you told them?" I asked softly.

"I don't know where she's gone."

I took the empty glass from her. "And that was when they hurt your arm?"

"Yes. But not very much. Not too much."

"Doris," I said, "have you got any friends you could visit?"

She got to her feet and smoothed her skirt. "And leave you to look after yourself, Mr Mallin!"

"Of course not, Doris. I didn't think. Now, how about a sandwich or something?"

Which was how we came to be sitting together in the kitchen and didn't hear the cars arrive. There was a hammering on the front door, and Doris made for the hall.

"No, I'd better go."

She looked at me doubtfully. "They wouldn't have come back?"

"They wouldn't hammer on the door," I told her, and went to open up.

Shri Ravat was standing on our doorstep. Behind him, in a ragged arc, was his gang of supporters. In the town I'd been able to accept them, but here, standing against a backcloth of Salop sky with the hills forlorn beyond, they were so incongruous that I nearly laughed. Ravat was very nearly sensibly dressed — his black leather jacket with the sheepskin collar — but below the waist his slacks were flared like a skirt, were short, and revealed his chunky platform shoes. But he was conventional compared with the *farago* who trailed at his heels. Fringes, beads and patchwork colours prevailed. The one with the goatee beard carried his guitar.

Behind them was their transport, a clapped-out 2.4 Jag and a retired city taxi painted in psychedelic glory. I'd not thought of them as having their own vehicles, but they couldn't have stolen them. Not even they could have stolen such wrecks.

"We have come for Toni," Ravat said fiercely.

"She isn't here."

"Then we come in to look." He moved forward.

I stepped in front of him. "You should have brought your portable welder. Without it you're nothing. Now go away."

He looked at me plaintively. "I invited you to my home."

I saw only one way to get rid of him. I grinned because it was becoming difficult not to laugh.

"Then, my dear friend come along in. Look where you like. Be my guest." I stepped back.

I had, actually, meant Ravat alone, but they took it as a signal and crowded forward, and though I shouted: "Heh!" all it produced was a lifted stetson from a pallid and fat person with a cigar stuck in painted lips.

Then the thing went beyond me. Ravat searched the house, but the others lost interest and wandered free. I'm not sure whether their scorn at worldly possessions lost out to their animal desire for comfort, but half an hour later I realised that I wasn't going to get rid of them all that easily.

The trouble with the young is that they cannot sustain an intention. Very soon most of them had forgotten what they'd come for. The Oriental was explaining to Doris the correct way of frying rice, whilst two of the others — no, three; things have changed — danced to Doris's radio, and I was just in time to prevent goatee beard from recording a love song he'd composed to Elsa's photo on the mantel. I've since wished I'd let him go ahead with the cassette deck.

I realized suddenly that these people were quite capable of simply moving in. To stay! Ravat alone was unamused. He'd found my store of spirits and was drinking himself into a sullen fury. So I went and found the Colt in my motoring coat and pressed the muzzle against his kneecap.

"Ravat, you will now please take your friends out of here."

He stood up with dignity. "If you have touched her, personally I will see you dead."

Then I was aware that the house was silent and the mood had changed. They were all in a grim circle round me, and I noticed again how very large they all were. But Ravat made a gesture. They turned and went out.

I watched them from the door. The Jag tore shreds from the drive, the taxi clattered, and they drove off jeering and waving fists. Then I returned to calm Doris, who was close to hysteria. She knew how to fry rice, anyway.

It had been a tiring day, so I went to bed early, intending an early start, but you know how it is. I woke to the postman's knock on the front door.

"A parcel," said Doris as I trotted down the stairs in my dressing-gown. "I've left it on the table."

The table to which she referred was the small one in the hall, and the phone beside the parcel rang as I was examining the postmark. The package had been sent first-class mail, posted in Birmingham at 3.30, but all the same Dainty was being a bit optimistic, I realized when I heard his voice, to be phoning so early.

"Got your present, Mallin?"

"Got it but not opened it."

"You know what it means?"

"Perhaps it's my birthday." And I hung up, cutting off what I expected to be a nasty laugh.

Then I opened it carefully; my

copper's instinct. It was a handbag, a leather, plain, blue handbag.

"Doris!" She put her head in from the kitchen. "Come here a second, will you."

She came, and I held it up. She didn't need to speak because her hand went to her mouth.

"Elsa's?"

She nodded. "But she didn't take it with her. She left her blue suit, and it's not the season for white gloves."

"White gloves?" I didn't get that. But I was too busy looking inside it. All it contained was Dainty's stupid note.

So now you know we've got her. You know what that means. I want the girl, killer.

It was all too pitifully obvious. The two trogs had taken the bag with them the day before, and they'd hoped to con me with it into believing that they had Elsa.

"But they didn't take *anything* with them," Doris protested.

144

"They'd toss it from the bedroom window to their friend in the car."

"I didn't see a car."

"There's *always* a car, waiting, engine ticking over for a fast getaway. It's instinctive behaviour."

I'd have laughed at the paltriness of the trick, except that it had a bitter flavour. The intention was there, you see.

"But there's a car now," Doris said, and she opened the door to Flagg and Lew Braine.

It's a good time to call, before your victim's had his breakfast and when he's still dazed with sleep. But it would have meant an early start for them, and Flagg himself was drained with lack of sleep. He seemed to shake himself as he marched in, jerking some action into his tired brain.

"Mallin, I'd like to search this house."

"If you have a warrant you'd demand to."

"I believe Miss Brent may be here."

I smiled. "If she was, you could take her. I'd rather you had her than Petrucchi."

Lew Braine was not looking at me. He was looking at the handbag and its wrapping paper. His eyes were keen.

"When you're working for him?" Flagg snapped.

Dainty didn't realize it, but he'd dealt me a useful card. I tried it for size, wondering how far I could bluff Ins. Flagg.

"But all the same, he's doing some demanding of his own," I told him. "Only he's got something better than a warrant. He's got my wife."

Flagg went very still. Up to that moment he'd imagined that he could achieve anything with his authority and his anger. But maybe his personality could blunt itself against a frightened man, and I was looking suitably afraid.

"I don't believe that," he decided.

I showed him the bag. He took out the note. "Killer?" he said. His eyes met mine. "Killer!" he cried.

"It's a personal joke. I know the man who wrote that." Perhaps I haven't a poker face. Flagg eyed me disparagingly.

"But you don't believe they have her?"

I shrugged. "The bag's empty. They could have got it easily, and if Elsa had had it with her they'd have left her stuff in it, if only for effect."

"So you know where your wife is?" he demanded.

"No, I don't know where she is. I'm just sure Petrucchi hasn't got her."

"Then what the hell're you talking about?" he shouted. "First one thing and then the other. Here, take it. It means nothing."

"It may mean something," Lew Braine said quietly.

Flagg whirled on him. "What?"

"That our friend here needs to prove that he hasn't taken the girl. If he had — he wishes to infer — then Petrucchi would know. So Mr Mallin pretends that Petrucchi does not know where

147

the girl is, and that Mr Petrucchi is angry about it."

I watched him with admiration. "So?"

"So you posted the handbag to yourself."

"Knowing that you gentlemen would be calling to search the house?" I asked.

"Which we haven't done," cut in Flagg angrily. "Let's get on with it."

"Without my permission?" I said gently.

Flagg growled deep in his chest. I thought he was going to push me aside and march through. Lovely. I could have phoned the police. But Braine said:

"Knowing that we'd search the house, you wouldn't have her here. So we'll go away."

I laughed. "Oh no, come on in and help yourselves."

Which they did, and incidentally found the tie-pin I'd lost a month before. In gratitude I gave them coffee and egg and bacon, which Flagg ate with violence and with dreadful hunger. He sat back finally, stared at me with bleary intensity, and belched mightily. He raised his eyes slowly from his cup, and returned my affronted stare balefully.

"I want that girl, Mallin," he said.

"Even with her, you've got no case, and you know it."

"And I intend to have her." He pointed the cup at me. "So don't try to confuse the issue."

"It *is* confused. You're not blind, you're just refusing to look."

"We'll be leaving now."

"What is it you want?" I shouted. "Arturo? D'you think he'll toss himself into your lap?"

He stood up, put the cup down blindly so that it smashed to the floor, and didn't notice.

"You'll bring the girl to me," he told me. "Soon, Mallin, soon." He nodded, looked unseeingly at Doris, and led the way out. Then he came back. "And

149

Mallin, you'd better find your wife, just to be sure. You understand?"

And finally he left. I waited until the engine note had completely faded — but the uneasiness remained. Something terrible had happened to Flagg when his wife had died. Before, he'd been determined to get Arturo Petrucchi; now, nothing was going to stop him. Nothing like reason and logic, nothing like normal human behaviour.

It had been stupid to ask Elsa to leave without telling me where. I'd feared violent action from Petrucchi, but he'd no more be able to get Elsa's address from me than Toni's.

"Doris," I said, "where has Elsa gone?"

"I told you, Mr Mallin, I don't know."

I tried again. "I know you've said she didn't tell you. But you were standing here, and you saw that man. You heard him. I need to *know* that Elsa's safe."

She sat down opposite me at the kitchen table. "Of course she's safe."

"Then you know?" She shook her head. "You must have an idea." But she was unresponsive. "Think, Doris. From what she took. From what she said."

"She could have visited a friend. A relative. Or even gone to stay at an hotel."

"In the winter?"

"There's places she's very fond of."

"Doris," I said, "I want you to get a piece of paper and write down every possibility. Everyone. Miss nothing out."

And good Lord she did. I've never known anyone with so many relatives as Elsa. They made a sizeable list. I stared at it in dismay. "This is the lot, I hope."

"There maybe people I don't know about."

So I sat with the phone in the morning-room and ploughed through it. Directory Enquires were kept busy. Uncle Albert? He was in America. Cousin Rachel? She turned out to be

151

at St Moritz. Aunt Vera? But she'd had a difference of opinion with Elsa earlier in the year, over some curtains if I recalled correctly. And so on. I went through the lot. Either they were away from home, or they hadn't seen Elsa. Much as they would have liked to, they all said.

The only slight hesitation I detected — it was no more than that — was from Aunt Vera. "Is that David?" she asked, and it was only when I'd admitted it was that she went on to say that Elsa was not there. But it was so small a hint, and after all she could well have cherished a dislike for me. It was partly because of me that Elsa had rushed away from there, leaving Aunt Vera to decide on apple-green velvet, or whatever it was, for the curtains in the morning-room.

So that, after two hours on the phone, I'd discovered no more than a hint. I'd tried four hotels. There was only one left. Doris had put: a little place on the Lakes.

"Doris!"

She appeared so quickly that she could have been listening anxiously just outside the door.

"This place on the Lakes," I said. "Don't you know its name?"

"All I know is that she loves it there."

"Isn't there anything . . . "

"There's a picture in her scrap album."

We searched it out, and eventually found the photograph. I'd hoped it would include an inn sign, but there was no such clue. "Which lake?" I asked. "Do you know that?" She shook her head. I tried a few. "Windermere, Coniston, Ullswater . . . "

"Ullswater," she cried. "I'm sure it's that."

I looked at the photo doubtfully. It was a small and delightful hotel, the water shown beyond it, mountain ranges beyond that. I could understand Elsa's enthusiasm for it, but the Lake District is over two hundred miles from

Shropshire, and there's the Kirkstone Pass between us and Ullswater, which was not a small consideration in January. I looked at my watch. Midday. Two hundred miles, plus the pass. Four hours, five?

I said: "Put me up a few sandwiches, Doris. And a flask of coffee. I'll take the photo."

And one of Elsa, just in case I had to go asking around, and it was while I was sorting one out that I discovered that there was a wedding picture of both of us missing from a frame on the dressing table. I hurried.

I was aware that I was racing against the light. If I was to find the hotel, I was going to have to recognize it. I held the Porsche on the legal maximum all the way up the motorway and by the time I'd reached Kendal I seemed well in hand. But it's always the last bit that's the worst. It had been raining all the way through Lancashire, and entering Cumberland it became sleet. The visibility deteriorated, the light faded. At Windermere they told me I'd be lucky to get through. There was a road patrol flagging down all drivers heading north. I waved and drove on.

Kirkstone Pass was terrible. Snow swirled and curtained in front of me. I forced the car onwards. There seemed to be no other traffic. The car behaved beautifully. I passed the Kirkstone Pass Inn at the top, rejected the thought of a rest and a drink, and began the descent to Patterdale.

There I just had to stop, because I had no idea where to start looking for the hotel, and it was already dark. I sat in a café and asked the waitress.

"Oh yes," she said. "Of course I know it. It's the Regency. Only about five miles from here." A detective's job is quite simple, really.

I'd never have recognized it. It nestled almost in the water, a small place but select. There was a car park, but no Rover in it. Hardly anything in it. I went inside, and was struck by a wave of warmth and welcome.

Partly, I must admit, the illusion was caused by the illumination. They had the foyer done in red, carpets, upholstery, curtains — and all the lights were red. After hours of driving and blinking into the white glare of the snow, the effect was almost soporific.

There was a sleek young man at the desk. He looked at my photo of Elsa. "No sir. Not the name or the person. I'm sorry."

I was terribly tired and the depression swept over me. "Can I get a drink?"

"It's rather early . . ."

But I wasn't listening any more. Lew Braine was standing just inside the entrance doors.

It could not possibly have been chance; he must have followed me all the way. Intent on my driving, I'd not troubled to check.

"No?" he said.

"You've come all this way to ask that?"

"I've come all this way to ask why *you've* come all this way," he told me.

"To look for my wife."

He shook his head slowly. "I suggest not. You want to persuade us that you're worrying about your wife, because then we shall assume that Petrucchi is angry with you for letting the girl slip through your hands."

My head was swimming. I hadn't thought Braine had been serious when he had put forward the same idea back at the house.

"I'd hoped Elsa was here."

"You knew she wasn't. Mallin, you're wasting your time. Flagg wants the girl, and you can produce her."

I said: "Petrucchi wants the girl, too."

"So you said. It's been a pleasant run, anyway."

I turned away and asked the receptionist to get me the house. Doris answered shakily.

"She's not here, Doris. Any news?"

"No sir."

I hung up and looked round. Braine nodded and walked out. The phone was as white as the register pages in the red light. I paid for the call and forgot I'd wanted a drink, and as I left I discovered why I hadn't noticed Braine following me. This was the first time I'd seen him with his own car. It was a TR6, and he was just edging it out of the car park.

Sitting in the Porsche, I examined my maps and located Aunt Vera's address. It was south of Windermere, and not too far off my route home. But I wasn't going to be able to avoid Kirkstone Pass, and if I didn't get going I'd be stuck on it, I realized.

I never did catch Lew Braine. It was still snowing, and the wind still tossed it around, making the visibility very poor. I was nearly into Bowness before I ran out of it. Then I found I could see, even the road signs, and I drew into Aunt Vera's drive at around eight.

I had never been there. Elsa had called it a delightful little house, and so it was, a delicate example of Regency taste, looking warm and inviting in its circle of trees. But there were no lights on. I didn't drive up to the house, but walked up. There were tyre tracks in the snow, which was only an inch-deep layer here.

I rang at the front, but there was no response, so I walked round the back.

There were some outbuildings, the ruin of a summerhouse, and a narrow terrace of uneven flagstones. But still no light. I tried a french window, but it was locked.

Then there was the faintest of sounds behind me, the soft crunch of snow under a heavy heel. I turned quickly, by instinct diving my hand for the Colt in my pocket. I got it out, but there was a whirl of movement in the air and something solid contacted just above my right ear.

I was aware, as my consciousness slipped from me, that I fired one shot. Unfortunately into the air, but nevertheless a shot.

8

I CAME round with a mouthful of snow and a realization that I had reason to be pleased. But my head throbbed and I couldn't trap the feeling, and when I discovered the french window was open I didn't think about it for a while.

The house was empty. Somebody had knocked me out, gone through the house, and left again. I must have been unconscious for a long time.

There was no trace of Elsa in the house. It was delicately furnished and there were indications everywhere of the careful and painstaking use of money. But not a hint of Elsa's presence.

That was when I finally captured that fleeting feeling of pleasure. I realized that if someone else was also looking for Elsa, then it did seem that Petrucchi didn't have her. But of course I had no real reason to suppose he did. My frantic chasing around had been provoked by the aura of fury surrounding Ins. Flagg.

And on the way home I unearthed another thought. How had they known of Aunt Vera's place? I determined to knock up Doris and demand to know, even though it was after two when I got back, but Doris was still up and waiting, and her face was so screwed-up with worry that I couldn't be too heavy with her.

"How could anybody know about Aunt Vera?" I asked. "You say you told them nothing."

"Well . . . " She moved uncomfortably on the kitchen chair. "There *is* Elsa's address book."

"Did she leave it behind?"

"It's not in the house."

I was drinking hot soup, my eyelids aching with tiredness. "How do you know that?"

"After you left I thought about it. So

I searched." She bit her lip. "Then, if you'd phoned, I'd have been able to give you any address we'd missed."

"So she could have taken it — or they did?"

She nodded. I had to be careful with Doris. Some of my tension was spilling over and affecting her.

"Well," I said cheerfully, "they haven't found her yet, and if we can't, nor can they."

She smiled weakly and went to bed, and I wasn't long after. I'd decided what to do about Doris. If she wouldn't remove herself from the house, then I would do so. If I was elsewhere, people wouldn't keep coming to the house to haunt me. So first thing in the morning I hunted out the old folding bed in the attic.

You'll realize at once that this precluded the Porsche. But the Dolomite isn't all that much bigger, and when Doris saw what I was up to she insisted on blankets and sheets, so it was all a bit of a struggle.

"I'll camp out at the office," I told her.

She had returned to the house, and I was edging the bed in the rear door of the Dolomite, when the car came up the drive. It was an ordinary police patrol car and I watched it with interest. Lew Braine got out on the passenger's side.

I was wearing my motoring coat at the time and the Colt was still in the pocket. Dainty's Smith & Wesson was at the bottom of the Severn. I didn't think the sergeant ought to know about the Colt.

"Help you in with that?" he asked.

"Thank you, I can manage." As I struggled I turned away from him, slipped the gun from my pocket, and thrust it down between the folded layers of the bed. As I turned back, the patrol car drove away.

"Your car's leaving," I said.

"I know. I thought you'd give me a lift, seeing that you're going to the station anyway."

Before I could question that, the postman arrived. I've thought about it since, and the only answer I can find is that he wasn't a postman at all. But you're fooled by the red bike, and they don't always wear their caps, and the uniform is only a mid-grey suit anyway. But what this postman had for me completely distracted me from his appearance, and if the stamps weren't franked I didn't notice.

It was a soft, floppy package, and inside was the silk headsquare that Elsa wore round her neck. Real silk. I bought it, so I know. It was printed with a soft green background and a design of white daisies, each with a different number of petals on it, with, round the edges, the French *crie de coeur*:

J'aimerai que les marguerites aient moins de petales.
Elles en seraint moins jolie, mais mon coeur seraint plus certain du tiens.

"It's Elsa's," I said quietly. Then I raised my voice. "Doris!"

She came running. There was no hesitation. "Yes, sir, she took it with her."

Then the accompanying note fell from the wrappings.

Next time, Mallin, I'll tie it round her neck. Tight.

"The old man wants to see you," said Braine, and I said, "right, right," thrust the package into his arms, him into the car, and scrambled in behind the wheel.

Braine said nothing at all on the way there. Perhaps he sensed my mood. I swung in the station yard and I was in front of Braine through that rear door.

Ins. Flagg sat in a chaos of paper, at which he was staring with bemused despair. He looked up as I entered and was perhaps relieved at the interruption because he was relatively mild with me.

"You've brought the girl?"

"You know damn well I haven't."
I snatched the package from Braine's
hand and threw it on the desk. "Take
a look at that."

He stood, one hand supporting him
each side of the square of coloured
silk.

"You know what that is?" I demanded.

"My wife had a similar one." He
looked up at me, his eyes haunted.

"Then you know what the words
mean?" I asked.

He shook his head, went on shaking
it as I sat down, as though I was
demanding the impossible.

"This is your wife's?" he said at
last.

"It is. She took it with her when she
went away. There's no doubt about
that. You know what that means!"

His eyes went vague. "I bought it for
her in Paris, on our honeymoon." Yet
he had not known the meaning of the
words.

I sat down slowly and glanced at Lew
Braine. He smiled without humour. We

waited. Flagg's head finally came up and he tried for a smile himself. It revealed his teeth but no more.

"Yes, I think I can see through this," he said. "She's been moving around. perhaps she's trying to keep one move ahead of you Mallin." His voice was hard with pain. "She must have left it behind at one of her stops, and it's fallen into someone's hands."

But I didn't want to accept that she'd ever leave it behind. It had a special meaning for both of us — I'd always believed.

"Can you translate the French?" I asked. He shook his head, so I obliged.

"'I could wish that the daisies had less petals. They might not be so pretty, but my heart would be more certain of yours.' Do you still think she'd leave it behind?"

"Women are notoriously unsentimental, Mallin."

"You think she would?" I insisted. He made no response. "Would your wife have done so?"

He slapped his palm hard on the desk, one brief movement, and then was still. Braine's chair squeaked on the floor.

"It's obvious *your* wife did," Flagg said icily. "Petrucchi's men got the scarf but not the woman. So why, if he sent it, would Petrucchi want you to believe he is holding your wife?"

"Because he thinks I've got Toni Brent somewhere. He's trying to force my hand." Was the man dim or something?

"Tcha!" he cried in disgust, and he swept himself to his feet, the chair flying wildly. "And why the hell'd he want the girl? Tell me that. A swap? Person for person — and then he'd hold the girl himself. Then why?"

But I was out of my depth there, because it was something I couldn't understand. "He expects her to change her evidence," I suggested, but not with too much faith.

"Then he thinks I've got a good

case?" Flagg demanded.

"I don't know what he thinks. But certainly his brother would be safer without her evidence."

"Yes!" he shouted. "Bloody exactly. You heard that, Lew! So what Petrucchi really wants is the girl removed. Permanently."

"No," I said.

Flagg laughed hideously. "But of course he does. It's the quickest, surest way of suppressing the evidence."

And because I couldn't understand Petrucchi, I was unable to make my point forcefully enough.

"It wasn't what he said."

"When you saw him?" His bushy eyebrows probed at me.

"Ask anyone who was there."

"But of course he'd say that," Flagg claimed. "For the record. And he'd leave clever Mr Mallin to get his meaning."

"I pretended — "

"And you did get his meaning!" he roared. "Don't lie to me. You got his meaning, and you agreed."

"It was a — "

"Contract!" His fist slammed down on the square of silk. "I know. I've had him in here."

"Petrucchi?"

"Keller. Dainty Keller. He was there, and he heard you. You waved a gun and you said you would remove her."

And sneering, his eyes alight, Flagg advanced on me and thrust his face close to mine. I was aware that Braine stood behind my chair. Flagg's hand closed on my shoulder, his fingers dug into my flesh.

"A contract, Mallin. A contract fulfilled."

I had to take a deep breath, even though it meant inhaling the spent air from his straining lungs.

"You don't believe that."

"I believe you killed her," he said savagely.

And all I could do was shrug.

His eyes searched mine, and slowly they went out of focus. It was as though his brain had drawn a curtain. There was spittle on his chin. He straightened suddenly and turned away in impotent fury.

"But if I'd killed Toni," I said, "why should Petrucchi threaten me by getting hold of my wife?"

"I'm not accepting that," Flagg said, calm now. "I don't think he's threatening you at all."

"But he sent me her headsquare."

"Did he?" he sneered.

"Somebody did."

"You — perhaps."

"How the hell . . . Doris says she took it with her. Braine heard her say it. She had no time to make anything up."

"I heard her," said Braine quietly. "I believed her."

"So all right!" Flagg shouted, letting go again. "It could still be your idea. You know where your wife is, so you get in touch with her and you ask her to send you the headsquare. Don't try your tricks on me, Mallin."

"But why?" I appealed. "Why would I do that?"

Then abruptly, frighteningly, he switched character and was laughing, a kind of hoarse bellow. "Because you think you can bluff me. But you can't, Mallin. You've killed the girl, so naturally you'd like me to believe she's still alive. Oh yes, that's very important. So you try to persuade me that Petrucchi knows her to be alive. Because — believe me, Mallin — Petrucchi wouldn't be caring a tuppenny cuss if he knew the girl was dead. So you try to persuade me that he does care a tuppenny cuss, and you do that by fooling around, pretending that Petrucchi is either after your wife or has got her already. How does that sound to you? Have you got me fooled?"

I felt hot with nausea. "The headsquare — "

"This?" He picked it up, balled it in his palm, and threw it at me, but of course it ballooned open and drifted gently against my face. "Don't you think, if *he'd* sent it, that it would have had blood on it? He couldn't have resisted the temptation. Hers — or somebody else's. There's plenty of blood where Petrucchi lives. So — where's the blood?"

He suddenly roared out at me. "So go and get me some blood, Mallin. Or bring me the girl. Bring me something, if it's only your wife's body. Because maybe, then, I'll believe that Petrucchi's got her."

I turned and looked at Lew Braine. Gently he shook his head. I didn't know whether it was a refusal to help, or a warning to accept things as they stood. I took the headsquare out of the air and moved to the door, wondering if Flagg would let me go. But of course he would. It was Toni he wanted, and only I could produce her for him.

With one sentence I could have explained about Toni, but my reason in hiding her in the first place had been to keep her from Petrucchi. The police would release her to the general view. But now I was not convinced — not absolutely and finally — that Elsa was safe and well. So now I dared not speak.

I turned and walked out of the room, got in the Dolomite, and drove with my bed round to the office. I parked, leaned behind and transferred the gun back to my pocket, and only then troubled to look around to see if I was observed.

One big black car waiting would have warned me. Two would normally have sent me romping away from there, but Dainty was in the entrance shadows, and his hands were in his coat pockets. I got out of the car. You don't want trouble if you can avoid it.

"Visitors?" I asked politely.

He jerked his head and we began to climb the stairs.

"Good of you to tell the inspector that I killed the girl," I said.

"Insurance," he said from behind me.

"I'll remember. I may ask for a premium."

I didn't get a chance to use my magic pen. They'd jemmied my door, ruining my lovely lock, and simply so that Petrucchi could wait in comfort, sprawled in my chair.

"Crummy dump you've got," he said, and Dainty relieved me of the Colt. He tossed it in his palm.

"Fair exchange," he decided.

Petrucchi had brought four other men with him, as Dainty had brought Slim. Any pair of them would have fitted Doris's description as ugly.

"I don't journey out for anybody," said Petrucchi, using a jack-knife to cut notches in the edge of my desk. "Usually they regret it."

"I'm not pleased," I admitted.

"You know what the scarf means?" he asked.

"She called it a scarf?" I asked.

He looked at me, the knife still.

"Or do you call it a scarf because she had it round her neck?" I demanded.

The point of the knife moved in a small circle in the air. "She called it a scarf," he decided, as the most likely.

"You're a liar. It's a headsquare. She'd never call it a scarf."

He snarled and stabbed down hard with the knife. The blade snapped. "Don't play games with me," he screamed.

"You pretend you've got her. And what have you done to prove it? You've sent me a handbag that your yobs stole from the house. You've sent me a headsquare they found trying to catch up with her. But it's nothing personal. Where is she, if you've got her?"

"Would I be so stupid — "

"At the house?"

"I'd be a fool."

"But you are a fool." He was half-way to his feet. "You want your brother cleared, but the police've got no case — I know that, Petrucchi — they've got no case, even *with* the girl's evidence. So why've you gone mad to get hold of her? She doesn't matter."

"I've got your wife," he insisted stubbornly. "I'll exchange her for the girl."

"Don't you understand! The girl doesn't matter."

"She matters to me. I want to make sure she gives the evidence I want her to give. So I'm holding your wife . . . "

"Then let me speak to her." I gestured towards the phone. "Dial them, wherever she is."

"Your phone's tapped."

"We can go out to a phone booth. There's one just round the corner."

"No." He thought about it, then bounced to his feet, appalled at the thought of such an undignified procedure. "No, I will not. What do you need to convince you, Mallin? Her screaming voice on a tape? But you'd say it was mine. Yes, I can scream." He did so. I stepped back. "Whatever I do, you'll deny or argue away. Shall I send you an ear? You'd pretend to believe it was Slim's."

Slim coughed anxiously in the background. I glanced round. The faces were stiff. I was supposed to feel the same fear. I did. But it was fatal to reveal it.

"You name it, Mallin, and you shall have it. A finger? Would you recognize her finger?"

There is always a moment when everything rests on the next action. I could back away from his bluff, but he would pounce in and carry it further . . . and further. But I'd already matched his buffoonery once, and he'd caught me unawares with his response. Now, I had to go on. You'll admit that. I had to try and find a confident laugh.

I laughed. To them it might have sounded convincing, but to me it was agony.

"A finger?" I said easily. "Well yes, I'd recognize that. Provided it was wearing my engagement ring."

But I was dealing with a professional crook. Petrucchi didn't have Ravat's native dignity, nor his magnanimity. Like a spoiled child, he couldn't bear to lose. He was immature, which, I suppose, is the main requisite for all good crooks. And in losing this small game of bluff he could find nothing to fall back on but his buffoonery.

His eyes slid past me and focused on Dainty. "You hear that? A finger. That's what he wants. So let him have it. Or even two."

And then, ridiculously, he jerked two fingers at me in what I believe is known as a Harvey Smith, laughing behind his empty eyes. And all around me the goons did likewise, cackling their cold amusement. They hated me for provoking this disturbing display. And only Dainty failed to join in. He did not laugh. His eyes were on his master with contempt, and then he opened the door for Petrucchi to lead the way out, for the goons to follow, for Slim to trip over Dainty's feet on the way past, so that in the end there was only Dainty remaining to leave. The laughter had cut off as soon as Petrucchi passed the door. Dainty smiled. He shook his head.

"Oh Mallin," he said softly, "you're backing a very weak hand. Don't call *my* bluff, or you'll regret it."

The door closed quietly. I sat down. The chair was still warm. I ran my fingers along the notches Petrucchi had cut. They were neat, precise notches. Only Petrucchi's lack of control prevented him from being as deadly as Dainty.

I picked up the phone. Petrucchi had said it was tapped, and he'd know. I spoke without dialling.

"No need to record this — I'm not calling my wife. Just tell the inspector that I can't produce his witness. Just can't."

I hung up, and stared at the phone. My nerve was going.

9

AFTER I'd been down to fetch the bed and the bedding my legs weren't too good, either. Opened out, it all looked incongruous in the office, but as things turned out I didn't get to suffer it.

On my last trip I'd brought up the maps, and with these and Doris's list I sat down to work out a route. There was nothing left that I'd failed to check, but it did occur to me that four hotels had denied knowledge of Elsa Mallin, but it may well have been that she'd made a thorough job of it and used another name. I didn't care to think that she might have used another hotel, too.

The four I had already checked, but only by phone, were near Cromer, the Forest of Dean, Bournemouth, and Bexhill on Sea. A brief glance at the map will show you that they can be encompassed in a neat circular run, in the order Gloucestershire, Hants, Sussex and Norfolk, though London will intervene between the last two. But I had hopes that I wouldn't need to try the last, because if I did the round trip would run out at around six hundred miles.

I looked at my watch. It was 11.22. There seemed no point in hanging around. I looked back from my busted door, hoped someone might pinch the bed, and got going.

Nobody seemed to be following me out of Birmingham, though neither Flagg or Petrucchi dared to allow me to run free. But in the traffic I was unable to pinpoint any specific vehicle, and once out on the open road I got down to some serious motoring, and not many people could have tailed me. It was because of this that I deliberately avoided the motorway, because you can't dodge them there, not realizing that my attitude was quite foolish.

What did I care who tailed me?

A little south of Worcester I became aware that I *was* being tailed, and rather surprisingly by a battered 2.4 Jag. I had thought that Ravat was waiting peacefully somewhere in the background. But he was not, and he was far from peaceable. His anger was enough to boost his driving nerve, though not his ability, and he drew up on me. I reckoned I could leave him standing; that Jag's engine must have been about to leap from its frame. But I wanted to know his intentions. I therefore allowed him to draw level.

This was the day Elsa's Dolomite got scratched. I felt him swing in to me, the Dolomite lurched, and I corrected a skid. The verge was a deep ditch. It looked very close to my near-side wheel. To have slowed then would have been disastrous. I held the speed, watching a far corner coming up. No traffic. The Jag swung away from me, using all the road. I waited until I saw his nose begin the next swing. Then I slammed my foot hard down on the throttle.

Even at eighty the Dolomite's got a lot of spare, with that single overhead cam of theirs. The seat hit me in the back, the exhaust roared, and I felt just a touch at the rear as he contacted. The car slewed, and then I was clear. I eased up and looked back.

The Jag was in the ditch, nose down, and somewhat crumpled. Ravat climbed out from behind the wheel. I think he'd taken my advice. Anyway, he seemed to be waving his welding torch.

I hoped he'd brought his gas cylinders, then he could possibly weld the Jag together again.

For a few minutes I was happy, but at the hotel near Symond's Yat they did not recognize Elsa's photo.

I had a quick sandwich and a half of bitter, and got moving again. There was a black car in the corner of their car park, but it didn't have to mean anything.

Then I realized that I would prefer it to mean something, because I'd rather have had Petrucchi's men behind me. Ahead of me, they might reach Elsa first. Then I realized that Petrucchi could probably command a number of cars, and though one might now be behind me, others — one possibly containing Dainty — could well be ahead. The engine note gradually rose. I whipped over the Severn bridge and settled the nose for Bournemouth.

I was tired, and the Dolomite Sprint is a car that needs driving, not simply pointing. Once or twice there were tricky moments on cornering, and several times I scared the hell out of other motorists by overtaking unwisely. I forced myself to ease down, and drove into Bournemouth at a reasonable speed. I found the hotel almost at once.

It was there I saw Lew Braine. Well, it was a TR6 in the same off-white, and driven by somebody very like him, but driving *away* from the hotel. I hope you realize what that means.

I almost ran into the foyer. I showed my photograph, asked my question, but no, she was not staying there. I said:

"Somebody asking, was there?"

His eyes flickered. He looked away. I produced my driving licence. "I'm the lady's husband."

"A gentleman did ask. Ten minutes ago."

"He had her photograph?"

"Yes sir."

"Then you should've recognized me," I said angrily. "I was on it, too."

"No. Nobody else was on it. Just the lady."

I went and sat in the car, terribly disturbed. It was obvious what had happened. Doris's nerve had gone, and when Braine had asked her she'd given him the same details as she'd given me, and another picture of Elsa into the bargain. It meant that it was Dainty who'd got the wedding picture with both of us on it from the dressing table. And her address book?

I left Bournemouth with less decorum than I'd used entering it.

Other implications forced their way into my mind, endangering my driving. Flagg! He'd declared himself unconvinced that Petrucchi held Elsa. But he would perhaps play safe and check. Yet if he'd decided on that, he'd have used the normal police channels, rapidly and efficiently. So why should he send Lew Braine — if it was not Braine's own idea — on ahead of me? Behind, I could understand. He'd naturally wish to know if I found Elsa, then he'd know he had a good chance of using his witness again, if only because I would have called off what he insisted on believing to be my bluff. If I didn't find her, he would know he was in trouble.

But in any event, whatever Flagg's reasoning, it was not logical that the sergeant should be checking ahead of me.

This was the coast road now, and I

took it as fast as the car would hold the road. But now the light was going, and I was having difficulty keeping my eyes open. There became too much of scrambling around corners, of screaming tyres and rushed traffic-lights. And I was aware that Flagg, or Braine, had short-circuited the difficulties of keeping ahead of me by having me tracked by radio car. There were far too many patrol cars parked on lay-bys. I couldn't drive faster than radio signals, but I tried.

I tried so hard that I attracted the attention of police cars apparently not in Flagg's confidence, who chased me to their boundaries, and radio-ed ahead for me to be intercepted.

This produced an interesting but hectic hour, because of course I couldn't afford to stop and waste time arguing. So I ignored them, swerving round cars that thought they'd provided a road block, and leaving flicking blue lights behind in the distance. The inevitable end was a tangle of patrol cars, half with orders to let me through, the other half determined to stop me, and while they sorted it out I went through on the grass verge, and took the very next left turn into the country.

With the result that I became lost. I was going too fast down minor roads to bear to stop and consult the map. It was now dark, and I nearly wept. I kept turning right, on the theory that I'd then reach the coast road. I did. I realized suddenly that I was on it, and that the sea was on the wrong side of it.

It was time for a rest. I swung into a roadside café, and nearly fell asleep over my second coffee.

Logically I should have stayed overnight at Bexhill on Sea. I'd had a lot of fast driving and little sleep in the past two days. But Braine put a stopper on that by leaving me a message at the Imperial.

She's not here, Mallin. Why not pack it in? You've made your point. I've checked ahead at Cromer, and she's not there.

There was a stirring of that anger that always gets me into trouble. The next stretch of the route was the worst, as I couldn't avoid London, and Bexhill to Cromer couldn't be less than 200 miles. It had also started to rain. Better than snow perhaps. But how could I *not* go to Cromer? How could I possibly trust him?

It was 7.30 and I made a firm attempt to calm the tension that was building up. I went for a good meal in their restaurant — but no wine — then started off again.

But London wasn't as bad as I'd expected. I don't know the city too well, but I kept to the outskirts, and they'd got it well sign-posted. Midnight found me on the Norwich bypass, and as far as I was concerned I was as good as there.

The night clerk disclaimed all knowledge of the residents, but as I appeared to be David Mallin, it so happened that he had a message for me. Would I phone a certain Sgt Braine? I assumed he meant at the station, and was right because Braine was there, as chipper as somebody just out of a shower.

"Mallin," he said, "I knew you'd be stupid and go on to Cromer. She's not there, you know."

"Is that all you wanted to say?"

"There's been a package delivered at your office."

"What's in it?"

He sounded hurt. "It's addressed to you. Rather a strange shape."

"Des . . . " I coughed to clear my throat. "Describe it."

"About four inches long, by an inch, by an inch."

I visualized it. The effort required to make the next obvious request made my head swim. "Please open it."

There were rustling sounds. My hand slipped on the handset. I nearly fainted with the heat in there.

"Mallin."

"I'm here," I said hoarsely.

191

"It's a lipstick. A lipstick in a gold case."

For a moment the reception hall swam before my eyes. A lipstick! My reading of Dainty's character needed revision. I could have understood his sending a package of the correct shape to frighten me, even that it should have contained a finger — any finger — but a lipstick! Surely he hadn't the imagination to perpetuate a joke. I panted, trying to recover, afraid that Braine would detect my emotion, not certain, even, what that emotion was.

"Not posted by me," I croaked.

"You could have done. The cancellation . . . "

I didn't wait to hear about the cancellation. Doris had said nothing about a lipstick missing. But Doris need not have known. I cut off, at once dialled the exchange, and asked for my home number.

The phone went on ringing. I gave it time, in case Doris was in bed, but it rang and rang emptily. I cut off, tried it again, and with the same result.

Now I was completely shaken. By that time I'd realized that a lipstick can be bought by anyone, but there was no possible reason why Doris should leave the house, or why she should not answer if she was there. Well . . . one possible reason.

I paid for the calls. "Is there an all-night filling station around here?" He directed me.

A full tank should have taken me all the way to Shropshire, but in fact it did not. It's a fast and open run across country, but there's a lot of gear changing and high revs. It drank the petrol, the way I was thrashing it.

There is nothing so lonely as a car at night on a deserted road. I was lonely and unhappy, and afraid.

I managed to find another all-nighter near Cannock. It was close to dawn. The chill hit me as I climbed from the car.

"Going far, sir?"

"Not far. Nearly there, now."

The sky was showing a touch of mauve behind the clouds when I drove up to the house. All the lights were on. A welcome. I got out of the car. One of Petrucchi's black fleet waited quietly beside the box hedge. So I knew what to expect.

Slim opened the door. There was no gun on show, but he smiled his tired, gentle smile. He gestured towards the drawing-room. I walked in.

Dainty lounged on the settee. Opposite him, neatly upright with her knees together, Doris was sitting, her face very still, a bruise on her right cheek. She looked at me. There was a message somewhere in her eyes, but I couldn't read it.

"Took you long enough," said Dainty.

"Sorry. I didn't know you were waiting. I hope Doris has entertained you."

"She's been very amusing," Dainty acknowledged.

"Do you find it amusing to beat women around the face?" I was trying to bring something to that hard, distorted mouth.

He moved one hand delicately, reached it out and took a fold of her skirt between finger and thumb, and gently moved them together, enjoying the texture.

"She was insolent," he said smoothly.

"And I suppose you've waited all this time to tell me that you're holding my wife?" I asked.

"I had to see you in person."

I went and poured myself a drink. I don't often drink, and it was a rotten time of day, but the floor was moving still with the motion of the car and my head was hammering. Without looking round I said: "You wouldn't strike her for being insolent, Dainty, because you wouldn't recognize an insult."

"I know a crack when — "

"I said recognize, in its meaning: accept. You're too big for insults. They flow past you."

I turned, the glass in my hand. I'd touched him. His feet were collected under him, tensed for a spring.

"So if you struck her," I said, "it'd be because she refused to tell you something, and that could only be where my wife has gone. So how can you claim to have her? You're a fake, Dainty."

He came to his feet. I drained the glass and put it down. Emptying my hands, in case.

"I sent you her lipstick, Mallin."

I shrugged. "A childish trick. You chose it because it was the shape of a finger. It doesn't indicate any subtlety."

"I didn't choose it. I took it from her." His eyes were very watchful and his voice steely cold.

"But it wasn't even her shade, Dainty. Really, you should pay more attention to details. A blonde wouldn't wear that shade."

"Oh . . . clever." He glanced past me, for Slim to register the point he was about to win. "When I know she's a brunette."

"Know?"

"Her photo . . ."

"Then you haven't even seen her?"

He drew in one long breath, and exhaled it gently. "And have you?" he whispered. "Recently. Are you so sure she hasn't bleached her hair?"

Doris suddenly spoke up. "Mrs Mallin would not, in any circumstances, bleach her hair."

He snarled at her, drew back his hand, then slowly lowered it.

"Petrucchi's got you worried, hasn't he?" I asked. "Don't you think he looks worried, Slim? What's the boss promised you, Dainty, if you fail? A quick death, or a slow one?"

"I'm not on the way to failing." He jerked his shoulders, settling the jacket more firmly. It hung lower on the right.

"But he's made threats in case you do?" I teased him.

"What *is* this?" he shouted. "What's with the questions?"

"Why does he need Toni Brent? It's

something I can't understand. Why does he *need* her changed evidence? What's the matter with no evidence at all?"

"Now you're being clever again. We know she's not dead."

"*I* know what she is," I said. "Do you?"

"You're a liar. You haven't killed her. That I know."

I smiled. My face was stiff with the concentration through the night. "But my gun was fired, Dainty."

He stared at me blankly.

"You mean you haven't checked!" I jeered. "Well, a fine gunman you are. You take my gun from me, and you don't clean it!"

"Fired?" His hand plunged into his pocket, and he produced the Colt. He glanced at me. He snapped out the clip and looked at it, jerked back the chamber to throw the shell from the breech on to the carpet, then peered down the empty barrel. He put it to his nose and sniffed.

"Fired," he agreed. "And you tell me that you used it on Toni Brent. Then you're a worse gunman than me, because she's been missing for days, and *you* haven't cleaned it, either."

"I didn't claim to be as good as you," I said modestly, and as he'd got the empty gun in one hand and the clip in the other, it seemed a good moment to hit him. Two days of misery and frustration went into that one blow, and as he crumpled over my fist a memory of Doris's bruise impelled the second blow, and then my temper exploded and as he went down and over the settee I plunged after, determined to kill him with my naked hands. I kneeled on his chest and drove my fists into his face, until there was a gentle cough just behind me, and the venomous end of Slim's Luger nudged me in the neck.

"Back off, Mr Mallin. Please."

I backed off. Dainty was still for a moment, then he gathered himself to his feet, stood with hunched shoulders, his head down, touched a handkerchief to his mouth and glanced at the blood, and slowly raised his eyes to look at me.

Slim coughed to draw his attention. "The boss wouldn't like it. Not if Mr Mallin couldn't move around."

Dainty had great self-control. Slowly he relaxed, he smoothed his lapels, smoothed his hair. "Later, perhaps, later." Then he gave Slim one of his deadly smiles. "You took your time."

"I was waitin' for you to cut him up, Dainty. Really."

"But you waited too long, little man."

He rescued the Colt from the floor and snapped the clip into it, jerked another cartridge into the breech. Then he turned to me again. "So now — all the clever words said, all the fine action completed — we can get down to business. That thing works, does it?" And he nodded to the hi-fi set-up.

I was quite shocked. Did he really want to march out to the strains of the dead march from the Eroica? "It works."

He drew his left hand from his pocket. He was holding a tape cassette. "You wanted to hear your wife's voice. Put this on. Side one."

Ridiculously my hand was shaking. There'd been such quiet confidence in his voice. I snapped in the cassette, pressed the Play button, and adjusted the volume. I stared, hypnotized, at the speakers.

It was Elsa's voice, clearly from both speakers. There could be no possible doubt of that. The hi-fi was of the finest quality, and it was as though she was in the room. It could not have been an impersonation.

'David, I may not be able to speak to you again. So please, if I mean anything to you at all, do what is necessary, and do it quickly.'

That was all. The tape hiss was very faint in the complete silence.

"And now what, Mallin?" said Dainty. "I want that girl. And I want her before midnight. You've only got to reach for a phone. I've written the number on your phone pad. Give me a call, and I'll go and get her myself."

And then he left, trailing Slim behind, and I never heard the car leave. Perhaps Dainty was driving, Dainty in his gentle mood.

The tape was running on. I reached over and switched it off. Doris stirred. "Sir, I didn't tell them a thing."

She'd had a bad night and must have been terrified. I did my best to find a smile. It wasn't much, but I think it got through.

"No, of course not, Doris. I didn't suppose you would."

"I'll get you something to eat, David," she said, and she went out blindly.

And when she came back with sandwiches and tea I did actually eat, though I had to force myself to swallow, but I couldn't offend her, could I, when at last she'd called me David.

By that time I'd run the tape

backwards, and forwards half a dozen times, trying to tell myself that it wasn't Elsa — although it was. The voice always started at 54 on my counter. I called Doris back as she was about to leave.

"Was that man alone in here, in this room?"

"Oh yes. For hours. That funny little one sat in the kitchen with me."

I nodded, and she left me to my thoughts. My head was buzzing but I tried to think. Again I played the opening of the message.

'David, I may not be . . . '

I switched it off. An idea was trying to force its way through the pall of weariness. Elsa had a habit of using my name quite a lot in conversation. You'll have noticed that. But there are different intonations, depending on where the name comes. I mean: 'David, I do wish you'd listen,' uses my name differently from: 'If you'd make up your mind, David, perhaps we could get somewhere,' and different again in: 'Are you coming to bed, David?' and the 'David' on the tape wasn't a sentence-beginning David, it was the one she puts between verbal comas.

All right, add this to the fact that the voice started at 54 and not at the beginning, that the cassette was the make I usually bought, and above all to the fact that Elsa had left — so surprisingly — without a message for me, and what did you get? You got the possibility (it was no more than that) that Elsa *had* left a message, on tape, and that Dainty had idly switched on and discovered what I'd missed. And, playing it through, he'd realized that he could make use of it by deleting part of the message.

My heart started beating again. Part? Which part? Not the end — *this* was surely the end of the message. But what sort of message, I wondered, could end with those words? I toyed with phrases, with words, I must confess, that I would have liked to hear.

'David, I love you, but I must go away . . . '

No. What about: 'I am going away, David, as you wished . . . ' Yes, she might say that. ' . . . because I realize you're involved in something unpleasant. I shall be longing to phone you every day, but I realize that would not be advisable.' Yes, she was intelligent enough to realize that, would probably say it. But how to lead in to what was actually on the tape?

'So I must hope that you can find some way to contact me, otherwise, *David, I may not be able to speak to you again. So please, if I mean anything to you at all, do what is necessary, and do it quickly.*'

Yes, oh yes. I called Doris. I told her my idea. She looked at me with swimming eyes.

"I'm sure you're right, David. Elsa would never leave without *some* message. She's so thoughtful. It's a bit like the cushion covers."

"What?"

"You know how she had that disagreement with her Aunt Vera over those apple-green curtains?"

Yes, I knew. Aunt Vera had been upset.

"Well," Doris went on, "it's not like Elsa to let a disagreement go on."

"It's not," I agreed.

"So when she started to embroider some apple-green cushion covers, I knew what she was up to."

"Doris," I said, "what are you getting at?"

"I've been wondering what's missing, and while I was sitting here, watching that horrible man crumple the seat covers, I realized. David, Elsa took the cushion covers with her. She *must* have gone to her Aunt Vera's."

I stared at her. But Elsa hadn't been at Aunt Vera's. No, but she could have been, earlier. And then left. Aunt Vera's! A chance left. Oh, dear Lord, another chance!

"Doris, I could kiss you."

And I caught her face in my hands

and kissed those crumpled old lips, and d'you know, they were as soft and tender as a teenager's.

"Now I wish I hadn't told you," she said.

I grinned. "Why not?"

"Because you're going to rush right out again, and you ought to get some rest."

I said: "I'll feel fine after a bath and a shave."

Which was as much time as I allowed myself, that and the half-hour I lost by dozing off in the bath, and the few minutes switching to the Porsche, because there'd been a moronic driver waiting in that car by the hedge, and he'd amused himself by letting down the Dolomite's tyres.

Which was why I came to be using the Porsche. Otherwise things could have ended differently, because anybody will hesitate before deliberately crashing their own car.

10

HAVING been there once, I had no difficulty in driving straight to Aunt Vera's. But now it was daytime. The trees around the drive were dripping drearily with the thaw.

They dripped on a maroon Cortina which I knew was Flagg's. I was too tired even to sigh.

I hadn't met Elsa's aunt before, but we knew each other at once, she from the wedding photos, and I because she and Elsa shared the same lovely eyes. But at that moment Aunt Vera's were suspicious and unflinching. She was over fifty, small and slim, and she was in a fighting mood.

"Come in, David," she said, cautiously friendly. "I'm pleased to meet you at last."

She offered a cheek and I kissed it. We were standing in a small, panelled hall, with a grandfather clock to the left of the door, to the right a small table bearing the phone. A man's overcoat hung on the hall-stand. I gave her my motoring coat to put with it.

"He's been waiting hours," she said as she led me into the soft and sensual room that had the apple-green curtains. Everything in that room was genuine and antique. Flagg was disturbingly real, and present.

He was sitting like a benevolent bullfrog in a satin-covered wing chair, and seemed too exhausted even to raise a hint of animosity. He drew himself forward on the chair arms with a vague gesture of standing to greet me.

"She's not here," he said.

"Then why are you waiting?" I asked.

"Expecting you. But she's been here, I'm sure."

"You're guessing. There was no reason to suppose I'd come here, either."

He shrugged. "It seemed logical. But

we reckoned you'd come straight from Cromer."

Aunt Vera lowered herself stiffly on to a Regency chair and laced her fingers on her lap. I took a seat on the settee that matched Flagg's chair. A cushion thrust itself into my back, and I drew it out. It matched the curtains, and was beautifully embroidered in a rose pattern. I tossed it to the other end of the settee.

"I was delayed," I said. "One of Petrucchi's men sent me a message, and I had to call in at home."

Flagg thrust his lower lip at me. "Is he still playing tricks?"

"Not convincingly."

"Ah! I take it he said he had your wife?"

"That's what he claimed. But he hasn't produced anything positive." I glanced at Aunt Vera, wishing to persuade her that this was serious. "There was mention of a finger." She caught her breath. "But it hasn't arrived. Do you drive a car, Aunt Vera?"

"Well no. I just don't seem to get the hang . . . " Her voice tailed away. She was not thinking about cars.

It was obvious, now, what had happened. The car tracks that I'd seen that night had been the Rover's. I'd missed her by no more than an hour, Elsa driving away, all packed, heading for fresh fields as I drove towards the house.

"But she's been here, hasn't she?" I said.

"I don't know what you mean."

I stood up. "Aunt Vera, I'm Elsa's husband. This gentleman is a police inspector. We'd both be very pleased to hear that Elsa's safe. Neither of us wishes any harm to her. So please say — she's been here, hasn't she?"

"Elsa and I had a disagreement," she said stiffly. "It's hardly likely she'd visit."

"It's very likely." I picked up the cushion and tossed it to her. "I like the covers."

Flagg stirred impatiently. "You're

wasting your time, Mallin. I've been at it for hours." He spoke with a ponderous dignity, as though he'd come to some irrevocable decision.

"They're very pretty," said Aunt Vera.

"How long have you had them?"

"Not long."

"I saw Elsa working on them two days before she left."

Her eyes were very dark and steady. "She sent them to me."

"By post? Did you keep the wrapping?"

"I wouldn't, would I?"

I turned away, disappointed. "Anyway, I'm glad you're pleased."

She relaxed. "Delighted."

"And that you patched up your quarrel."

"I thanked . . . "

Flagg sat up. I grinned at him. "*When* did you thank her?" he demanded heavily.

She shook her head.

"In your prayers?" His anger was

barely suppressed.

I smiled at her encouragingly. "It's all right. I know she left on the night your french window was broken."

"Damned women," said Flagg grumpily.

And Aunt Vera said: "How do you know about the window?" She'd avoided any admission that Elsa had been there.

"It's all *right*," I said. "She probably told you to say nothing, not even to me. But things have changed."

"I haven't seen her," she said clearly.

It obviously ran in the family, this stubborn and unswerving loyalty. I was very gentle with her.

"But if you hadn't seen her, you wouldn't know how important it is to deny it, in the face of all the evidence. The cushion covers, the tyre tracks in the snow that night. And the headsquare."

"What . . . headsquare?"

"Her headsquare has been sent to me as evidence that they have her.

213

They could only have found it here. But I need to be certain."

And at last I got through. Aunt Vera told us about it, composed still, but afraid. Elsa had driven straight to her aunt's, but had then decided to move on, as it was too obvious. She had not said to where, but she'd left a clue for David, if he should come asking, the headsquare in a drawer in her room. She had said that David would understand.

"Yes, I understand."

"That evening — she dropped me off at a friend's for dinner, and when I got back the french window was open. But I couldn't find anything missing . . . at first. Then I discovered the headsquare was gone. Nothing else."

"She didn't give you a hint of where she was heading?"

She shook her head.

"Hell," said Flagg, lumbering to his feet, "we're wasting time. I've had enough of your little act, Mallin."

"Act?" I demanded. "Are you still

pretending to believe that I set this up?"

His eyes moved angrily. "If you've killed my witness, Petrucchi would know it, so he wouldn't be interested in your wife. And if," he said heavily, "my witness is still alive, he wouldn't go for your wife, he'd go for you. He's got ways of persuading people that I can't use."

I was desperately tired, and worry swam in my head. But I kept my voice steady. "He wouldn't know I could tell him where she is. He could go too far, and then he'd never know."

"You're not that tough, Mallin."

"I wouldn't need to be tough, if I'd got nothing to tell him."

And then, slowly, he smiled. "So that, by frantically searching for your wife, you hope to persuade me that my witness is still alive, *and* that you don't know where she is. Both from the fact that Petrucchi's trying to find your wife."

"And you believe he's not?"

"There's nothing you've shown me to convince me he is."

"All right!" I shouted. "So *you* convince me my wife's safe. You've had men all round the country trying to find her. Go on. Try and tell me she's safe."

"And then you'd give me my witness?"

"I'd give you your wife's murderer, on a plate, chopped up fine," I cried, a little optimistically.

But I'd overstepped. For a while his subconscious mind had taken over from his over-strained brain, and had robbed him of the memory of his wife's death. And now I'd flung it back in his face.

"I've *got* the murderer," he shouted. "And I'm hoping to get the rest of that Petrucchi scum. So don't stand in my way, Mallin. I want my witness."

I took a deep breath. "Then first — for me — find my wife."

So that was his basic fact. Either find Elsa for me or convince me she was safe. And he was face to face with a desperate and weary man who'd just about had enough of words, and would only recognize facts.

"Look at it," he said, savagely probing for a fact. "Petrucchi's throwing paltry evidence at you, so obviously *he* hasn't got her. And if the whole police force can't find her, how can he expect to?"

"You think I'll be satisfied with that?"

"I don't see why not." He looked round wildly. "You had a row, and she went off. That's all it is."

"It isn't exactly how it was."

"It's happened to other men."

"I know Elsa."

"You know her!" he said with bitter scorn. "Since when did any man know his wife? You think you can trust her, you think you can depend on how she'll react — "

"I think that," I said angrily.

"Then you're a bloody fool," he cried. "What makes you think she doesn't *want* to stay missing? You tossed the chance right into her lap, you poor mug. Oh, she'd be loyal enough while you were watching her, but you sent her off on the loose — "

"What the hell're you saying?"

"I'm saying that you've been too gullible, that's what. You've taken her for granted, you've relaxed. You've assumed she would always want you. But who d'you think you are, something special? Who're you to take that for granted!"

Aunt Vera was standing, tensely appalled at his outbreak.

"I know Elsa loves me."

"Ha!" he cried. "Oh pretty — she loves you. Oh yes, they say that, and in their eyes there's the face of another man."

"That's impossible."

"Then where d'you think she is, all this time? Running around on her own? Oh no. They're all the same. Two days on their own and they're calling the boy-friend. Come for me, angel, I'm lonely. Safe? Sure, she's safe from

Petrucchi. She's probably on the Costa Brava right now with her fancy boy."

And he meant it. He felt it. Flagg was a person who could inject into himself any emotion he was expressing. He actually writhed in agony as he said it, and yet I knew he was talking nonsense. And then I knew why. I was close to cracking under the pressure Petrucchi was applying, and for his own sake Flagg had to remove Elsa, in my mind anyway, far from the clutches of Petrucchi's mob. If only into the arms of a hypothetical lover.

"Flagg," I said, "you're very good. You'd convince me if I didn't know about Elsa."

He was shaking with emotion. "Then why'd she leave the headsquare?" he demanded. "You and your fancy sentiments. Oh, it meant so much to both of you! But all the same she left it. Because she was leaving *you*."

Flagg was very smart, pouncing on it like that, and I had to oppose the suggestion without hesitation. And with confidence. Without looking at Vera I said:

"Aunt Vera, will you please tell him why she left it."

"Elsa said to tell David that the daisy she loved best has only one petal." She tossed it at him with poised dignity.

I shrugged, looking deep into his blood-shot eyes. "The 'I love you' daisy," I explained.

And then he knew he had lost that gambit. He growled, shook himself, and for one moment looked pitifully lost.

"And if," said Aunt Vera proudly, "Elsa had any thought of another man, why would *two* men come for her?"

"Two men?" I said softly.

"When was this?" Flagg demanded. He was suddenly dangerously quiet.

"Yesterday."

"And what did they do?" I asked.

"Asked some questions. I said I hadn't seen her."

"And they weren't violent?" It was strange, if they'd been the same ones who'd been violent with Doris.

"They suddenly laughed, and said never mind," said Aunt Vera, looking concerned.

"Never mind?"

I looked at Flagg. We both had the same hollow thought. Nobody says never mind unless they've got what they came for.

"Where were they standing — when they said that?" I asked.

"Why . . . in the hall. By the phone table — "

Flagg and I rushed for the door. I beat him by a foot. We ran to the phone table. There was a phone pad near the instrument, a pencil beside it.

"Oh no!" Flagg said hoarsely.

I snatched up the pad. The top sheet was blank.

"And I suppose," I said in disgust, "she left you a number just in case."

"No. Oh no," she protested.

"Oh yes," I almost snarled at her. "And you tore it off, stuffed it somewhere safe, and you didn't realize . . . "

"I didn't tear anything off."

But Flagg was already scribbling over the surface, bringing the last message up clearly. It was a phone number: Patterdale 235. I stared at it. Somebody was hammering inferences into my head. This had to be the hotel on Ullswater. And they knew! Dear God, they'd known since yesterday.

I grabbed at the phone, and Flagg's hand swooped to hold it down. His sweating face was close, his eyes quite mad. He couldn't allow me to know for certain that they had Elsa. Not for certain.

Furiously I swept an arm across his chest and sent him staggering. I grabbed up the handset.

Then Flagg charged at me. He was raging. All control of his actions had gone. It was the end for him if I knew. He ran into me and sent the table flying, the phone with it, and as I staggered back, caught completely by surprise by his action, he scrabbled his hand round for the wire and jerked it out of the wall.

"No!" he roared. "No!"

I got slowly to my feet. His action completely chilled me, because it meant he too realized what I'd hear. I said: "There's a screwdriver in my car," turned away, and went out to fetch it.

My legs seemed stiff and my head loose on my shoulders. I was vaguely aware of what I'd missed before; that Flagg had a driver waiting in his car. It was unusual to leave the man outside. Had Flagg suspected that he might have to use actions which he'd prefer another policeman not to see?

I returned with the screwdriver. He was standing with his back hard against the wall, breathing deeply. He made no effort to prevent me from unscrewing the fitting and replacing the wires. I sat the phone back on its cradle, removed it and got the dialling tone. I dialled exchange and asked for the number.

As I spoke I did not remove my eyes from Flagg. His face was stiff and unemotional. I could barely stand.

"Regency," said a man's voice.

"Have you a Mrs David Mallin registered there?"

"We had, sir. She left late last night."

My tongue was stiff. "I . . . this is her husband. Did she leave . . . alone?"

He seemed to pause, but maybe it was my racing heart that made it seem so. "Two gentlemen came. She left with them shortly after."

"Thank you," I said ridiculously.

"Will that be all, sir?"

"That," I said, "will be all."

I replaced the receiver. The screwdriver was still in my right hand. I dialled the exchange with it.

"No," said Flagg quietly. "I can't allow that, Mallin."

"You know what I've got to do."

"I know I can't allow you to do it."

I stared at him. A distant voice was saying in my hand, "Number please." I couldn't believe I'd heard him correctly.

"Put yourself in my place," said Flagg, his voice drawn from some hidden reserves of sincerity. "Imagine your wife was dead. As my wife is. You'd do *anything*. Do you think I can allow you to phone Petrucchi? I don't care what happens to me any more. So if you lift that phone to your ear I shall attack you. I know you've got the screwdriver, but that won't stop me. I'll attack you because I've got to stop you, and one of us may come out of it dead. I mean that, Mallin. So put down the phone."

The whole speech had been delivered in a droning monotone. The words had a certain insane falsity about them, and yet I realized that he couldn't have said anything else. It was inevitable. He would have to stop me.

Slowly I replaced the receiver. After all, Dainty had said I had till midnight. It was necessary to get away from the aura of this fraught creature.

225

He said: "That's better. I'm glad you can still recognize reason. Now . . . we'll take a trip in my car."

"What about mine?"

"My driver can follow on — "

"Not in my Porsche he doesn't."

"Very well," he said stiffly, "then you can take me in your car. Really, Mallin, you can be very difficult."

I went to say good-bye to Aunt Vera, whilst Flagg stood in the hall and watched through the open doorway. She was upset by the emotion and tension around her, and by the fact that there was now a real danger to Elsa.

"I've only got to make one phone call," I said, "and she'll be safe."

"David!" She reached out and touched my hand. "Elsa didn't leave me a phone number."

I didn't know what that meant. My head was buzzing from too many miles and too little sleep. I patted her shoulder and left with Flagg.

He got in the Porsche, settling his huge behind in the passenger's seat.

As I reached forward to switch on the engine, he said comfortably:

"All you need to do is give me two addresses, the one for Toni Brent, and the one where you met Petrucchi. As simple as that."

"You stupid great ape!" I said savagely. "He may not have taken Elsa there, he might not even be there himself. And you'd rush in like a herd of elephants, sirens blasting and blue lights winking. What sort of chance would that give Elsa?"

"As good a chance as you'd give the girl, if you handed her over."

I jerked the engine into life. He was wrong. Elsa stood no chance — but Petrucchi meant no harm to Toni. But then I realized what was really in Flagg's mind.

He had out-thought me, out-manoeuvred me completely, played me like a poor hooked fish. Hadn't Lew Braine said that Flagg intended to push Petrucchi into an error, then he'd have him! *This* was the error, the kidnapping of Elsa. Now Flagg had him. Eventually, he reckoned, I'd give him both addresses. Then he'd have both ends, the case against Camille, and the kidnap charge against Arturo. And if Elsa got killed in the process, then he'd have a murder charge against Arturo. It suited Flagg fine, just as long as he got those two addresses.

And I knew, as I drove from Aunt Vera's, that he did not intend to give me one chance to contact Petrucchi.

Not one.

11

THEN he had the infernal cheek to settle back in the seat and go to sleep. Did he have such superb confidence in his ability to control my movements?

Then, as I drove on to the M6, I noticed a patrol car observing me. But it went away as soon as I'd committed myself. The Cortina had been left behind miles back. There seemed to be no control of my actions at all.

I had to drive in at the first service station for petrol, and Flagg was awake as soon as the Porsche drew to a halt. He watched morosely as I filled up — though he made no effort to share the cost — and even followed me to the gents. Patrol cars were in evidence until I was firmly back on the motorway and heading south.

It was three o'clock. Very soon I was

going to have to leave the motorway. I woke him up.

"Where d'you want me to drop you?"

"Just keep driving," he murmured. He sat up and reached for his cigarettes. He'd had enough sleep. "You must be tired of driving," he said chattily.

Tired! I'd wake up with nightmares for the following month, seeing that road surface streaming back at me, feeling myself straining to keep awake — and, jerking awake, I'd still be in the nightmare of the roaring engine and the rushing wind.

"Take the next exit road," he said.

"It's not the one for — "

"The next one."

And a police car was neatly on my off-side wing, his indicator already flashing for a left turn. I took it, and the police car fell back. Another waited for me on the main road. Then they escorted me, one in front and one behind.

I wasn't going to have that. I let

them settle in for a couple of miles, then I did an abrupt right turn out of a signal junction, and put my foot down. Two minutes later one of them bounced in the rear-vision mirror, and far ahead I saw another easing out of a side road to precede me.

And so it was; so it continued to be. They nudged me, harried me, blocked me. I had no alternative but to wriggle my way across country — wasting precious time — as it became dark.

I slowed.

"Flagg," I said, "it's Sunday evening. Your case doesn't come up until Tuesday. Give me one day — just one day — to find my wife . . ."

"No!"

"Give me a chance, goddamn you."

"Keep driving," he said.

I slammed the gear into second viciously and tried to break his neck with acceleration. It didn't work.

"Next right," he said.

"Why're you taking me into the city?"

"That's where you left your bed. You may wish to lie on it."

"The office?"

He nodded. I drove there.

On Sunday evenings in Birmingham it's usually quiet. The orange street-lamps flood the pavements, and most of the shops leave their window lights on for the strolling dreamer. But off the main streets there's nothing but offices, and very few people are walking, even at five o'clock. Yet the block where my office is situated seemed strangely busy. Innocuous dark vans were parked on the far corners, and groups of indolent men stood in chatting groups.

I drew up in front of my office entrance. Across the other side of the street a shadow detached itself from a doorway, turned casually, and hurried away. I thought the face was Oriental.

Flagg got out of the car and stretched. "Any time," he said. "You pick up a phone and they'll connect you to me."

Then he walked away. I stood there,

a stubborn rumbling fury inside me. Then I jerked the motoring coat more tidily, set the rolled-brim hat firmer, plunged my hands into the side pockets of the coat, and began to walk.

Silently they closed in on me. "Excuse me," I said, and sidestepped into the gutter. Three heavy men confronted me. I shouldered them. "You can't do this."

They pressed in on me. "Sorry, sir."

"But you can't do it."

They took my arm firmly and turned me about. "I'm sorry sir, this way if you please."

"But you can't *do* it," I almost sobbed.

Gently they escorted me back to the office door. They nodded. They went back to wait.

I turned and entered and slowly climbed the three flights of stairs. It was ridiculous even to consider the phone. I pushed open the door.

"Your lock's broken," said Lew

Braine. "So I came in to wait."

"I know it's broken."

He was wearing his dark blue, belted raincoat and a cloth cap. He gestured towards my desk. "I've brought you some sandwiches and a flask of coffee. I reckon you haven't eaten for twelve hours or so."

"Very thoughtful. Do you realize what he's doing — what he's got you into?"

"It's quite clear," said Braine, his voice kind of distant. "He's going for the big prize, and he's going all out."

"I demand my normal rights to walk away from here unmolested."

"For the record?"

"The record," I told him grimly. "Just so that you won't imagine it's not going to include you. Because you can be damn sure I'll see both your heads rolling after this is over."

He indicated the sandwiches. "Cheese and tomato all right?"

I flung them in his face. He shook his head sadly. "You've got the wrong idea about this, Mallin. All you need to do is give us two addresses — "

"I've heard all that."

"This is a major operation. We've got the chance of pulling in all the Petrucchi crowd. Just give us this chance. Two addresses . . . "

"No. You'd got this all set up, waiting for me. Flagg didn't get an opportunity of phoning ahead, or using his radio. So he must have *known*, all the time he was waiting up at that house. He must have known they'd got my wife, and he must have intended to do this to me."

"Two addresses."

"Can't you understand what I'm saying? You're going along with the plans of a psychopath. He can't be anything else."

"I told you — I owe him."

"You can't owe him that much, whatever he's done for you. You've gone along with him all the way through, done whatever he wanted. You've been all over the bloody country, ahead of me and behind me, so don't tell me you couldn't have found my wife, if you'd wanted to."

He looked vaguely hurt. "I wanted to."

"But you weren't watching that hotel — "

"How could we have guessed . . . " he began sharply.

I cut him short. "You knew something about it. You were there that night when I reached it."

"But she wasn't there at that time. You know that. What's got into you, Mallin?"

But I was groping through a fog for an idea I couldn't grasp. Something was out of joint somewhere. He said:

"I waited while you checked she wasn't there. Then I saw you use their red phone — and then I left. There was no possible reason why we should check there again."

But Elsa must have been on her way from Aunt Vera's to Ullswater at that very moment. We must have passed each other in the snowstorm over Kirkstone Pass, when I'd headed for Aunt Vera's. I groaned.

"You've got to accept that you're beaten," he said.

"But I can't produce the girl."

"You can if you wish to."

"No." I half-turned away and looked out of the window. "Flagg guessed right. She's dead. I killed her." I turned back to him, pleading for his help. "So what can we *do*?"

"We never believed that," he said coldly.

"And now I'm willing to admit it. I'm desperate, Lew." But my voice was dead. I couldn't summon the enthusiasm that I usually employ when I admit to murder.

"So I take you in and charge you . . ."

"If you can only do something!"

"And you ask to see your solicitor, who just happens to be Morrison. Oh yes, very neat. But you didn't kill the girl, and you're simply trying for some way of reaching Petrucchi." He laughed softly. "Don't you realize why we haven't taken you in this evening, and held you for questioning? It's because we'd never have been able to prevent you from talking to somebody, somehow . . . "

"My rights."

"Which you know, I'm sure."

"Then you'd stick to the book?"

"We'd have to — at the station. Here it's unofficial."

"What you're doing . . . "

"Doing? Are we doing something?"

"All right," I said, gasping with the effort to remain calm, "then you can go to your bloody insane inspector and tell him no. No! I'd be throwing Elsa's life away to let him charge in like a mad bull."

"I'll tell him no."

"And keep away from me," I said in disgust.

He smiled distantly and turned to leave. "Pity about the sandwiches," he said, and I hit him as hard as I could behind the right ear.

He stumbled against the wall. I hadn't connected quite right. Lord, my accuracy was going. I hit him again, and this time he slid slowly down the wall and lay still.

It was the cloth cap that had done it; so distinctive. I jerked it off his head and tried it on. A little too big, but it would do. I rolled him over and stripped off the raincoat. No trouble there, except that I felt a twinge of nausea. I hadn't given him a chance.

Then I walked out, clattering down the stairs openly, trotted out into the street, and with no hesitation, as Braine would have done, turned left, away from the brighter lights.

I kept my head down, my eyes busy beneath the peak. The group watched me approach idly. A patrol car was parked opposite, its driver with his head back, his mouth open. I walked up to them — and overplayed it.

"Keep your eyes on the doorway," I said, and walked past.

I could feel eyes boring into my back. "Heh!" I did not look round. There were running feet. My nerve went, and I ran.

The first one took me with a flying tackle. One hand got an ankle and I stumbled, dragged myself free, kicked back at his face. The second one was coming up. I butted him in the stomach, then a whole hive swarmed round me, and I ducked down a side alley. Voices rang between the walls and hard heels resounded on the pavement. In the far light at the end, shadows moved. As I ran towards them they consolidated. A wall of heavy men stood between me and freedom. I hurled myself headlong into them, fighting and struggling and sobbing, but they were good men. The habitual hand on wrist and elbow held me, another grasped my other arm. I kicked out and a soft voice said, "Gently now, easy sir." And I knew that I had lost.

They led me back, handling me like delicate china. One wrong move and

I'd be shattered to pieces.

Lew Braine stood in the doorway rubbing his neck. I handed him the cap, and stripped off the raincoat. He nodded and put them on. "There's been a phone call," he said.

"Who?"

"He said he'd call again."

My legs dragged up the stairs. When I gave them assistance with my hand on the banister a pain ran up my right arm. I must have twisted it. I leaned in the doorway and looked at my office. Sandwiches were scattered all over the floor. I cursed my temper. The bed was against the wall, opened, blankets piled ready on it. Lord, I was tired. A dreadful desire to stretch on that bed swept over me, and nearly overcame me. But I did not dare to sleep. How many hours did I have? Six? But my watch had stopped. Time had stopped and the office was quiet, and against the wall the bed beckoned. My eyes were aching and heavy, and I craved sleep. I craved unawareness, just a short period of retreat from the agony and fear . . .

Savagely I attacked the bed, knowing I had to remove the temptation, but I could do no more than toss it around uselessly, expending energy. I left it crumpled on the floor and poured coffee into the cup of the flask and drank it, cup after cup, then lit my pipe and sat at the desk and tried to think.

But nothing came and the surface blurred, and when the phone rang my head was down on the desk surface, and I was not sure how long I'd been asleep. I snatched at the phone.

"So now you know, Mallin."

"Now listen, Dainty, I've got to tell you — "

"No." There was something wrong about Dainty's voice, a fear or a tension. "I'm doing the talking. We've got your wife, Mallin. You give us an address, or you get her back a bit at a time."

"Dainty, for Christ's sake listen. I can't — "

Then there was a click and another voice cut in.

"I'm sorry, Mr Mallin, but you certainly can't."

I slammed the phone down, missed the cradle, scrambled for it, and fell out of the chair. I was shaking when I picked myself up. The phone hung swinging by its line, swinging in and out of focus. I squeezed my eyes, reached for it, and managed to replace it. At once it rang again.

"Yes?"

"For your information," said the same man's voice, "I taped that last conversation. In case you'd wish to sue for threats."

"Thank you. Oh, thank you. What's the time?"

"Eight-seventeen, sir."

I hung up and went to look out of the window. The view was the same, quieter perhaps, but the same groups waited in both directions. No, not quite the same groups. A battered and now distorted 2.4 Jag and a psychedelic taxi were parked just outside the police ring. Just what I needed. Oh yes, indeed.

I put on the motoring coat and decided I ought to begin looking for ways out. Then because I might need something heavy, I slipped the big glass ashtray into my pocket. I went to look around.

The block in which my office lived is an old Victorian building, or group of buildings, of about four storeys. Mine, on the third, was about as high as anyone would wish to transact business. And it was all business, no private flats. The block was separated from its neighbours by a side road in one direction and in the other by an alley, in which I'd already encountered policemen. But if there were other business offices, there'd be other phones.

I explored. On the floor immediately below me there were two offices, one for a philatelist and one an importer. The nearest was the importer, and his assets couldn't have been very liquid

244

because he hadn't got a decent lock on his door. His frosted glass went unshattered; a shoulder against the frame sent the door swinging. By the reflected orange light I discovered his phone. I picked it up.

"I'm sorry, Mr Mallin, but we've got all the phones covered. Every one in the block."

I crashed it down again and walked out, leaving the door open.

There was no point, now, in exploring further possibilities of phoning. It was clear that I had to get right away from the building. Perhaps there was a rear entrance, I thought.

The foot of the staircase opens on to a wide lobby with a glass door into the front entrance porch. On one side of the lobby is an insurance agent. Nothing on the other side but a blank green wall. This left a gap beside the stairs, a dark and uninviting gap, and not only had I no torch, but also I didn't dare reveal the area of my activity. I felt my way along the wall, my feet moving in a litter of paper and cartons. I tripped over a rubber dustbin, then I reached the end and found a door in the side wall. I felt round it, located the knob, and turned it. The door was open.

It opened into more blackness, but there was a damp draught here and a scent of visiting cats. I groped forward. A wall, a period of nothing, further wall, a door. I paused. A door on my right. Should I explore? But my eyes were beginning to accommodate and dimly, almost as an illusion, I detected an orange-grey blur in front of me. I groped for it, tripped over something solid, stumbled forward, and realized that I was running my fingers over a window.

I had obviously reached the rear of the premises, so there should have been an outside door. Either side of the window. Left first, or right? I decided on left and began moving sideways. My fingers groped and fumbled, and then touched a frame, a shape. I reached quickly for where it should be, and put my hand on a heavy doorknob, beneath it a protruding key.

It must have been years since it had been turned, and it was now almost solid. I clamped a hand over my other fingers and groaned with the effort, and with a squeal the key turned. The knob was easier. The door opened inwards

Two men were watching the door opening. This was that blasted alley again. One of the men had blood on his face. He smiled invitingly. I slammed the door, and panted against it, with my darkness vision completely spoiled.

So then I had to find my way back, with my sense of direction gone, and almost gibbering at the loss of time involved. I found the window, turned my back to it, and headed forward, then remembered the door I'd passed on my right. Now on my left, of course. I put my hand to its handle. It turned easily.

There was a flight of stairs leading

downwards, and for some reason I could see them dimly. A cellar! And sometimes there are ways out of cellars. I moved as fast as I could down the stairs, and discovered why I'd been able to see. A line of light shone from beneath the door at the bottom. I opened it.

The cellar was large and chill. Against a side wall they'd fitted up a bench with equipment and a tape recorder. Seated at it was a uniformed man without his cap but wearing earphones. They weren't the sound-excluding type, and he heard me at once. He turned.

"Did you come for that tape?"

I made an angry gesture and began moving towards him.

"There's no point, Mr Mallin," he said with sympathy. "There's no way out of here. We checked."

I stopped. It was useless. "Aren't you cold down here?"

He grinned. "Perished."

I turned and left him, climbed the stairs, and felt my way out of the lobby. I went and had a look into the street. The groups seemed distant and blurred. I realized it was raining. There seemed a chance that I might make it into the building opposite, then I saw the faint glow of a drawn cigarette in the dark doorway. I turned away and began tramping wearily back up to my office.

It held nothing of comfort or inspiration, only the torment of the waiting bed. I moved on past my open door, to the far end of the landing. This was the first time I'd investigated this dark corner, but as I'd guessed there was another stairway there. I groped my way up. It creaked as though about to collapse, but it took me step by step towards the roof.

The landing above was smaller and narrower. Faint light penetrated through a skylight heavily encrusted with dirt. I searched for doors and discovered three. The first one I tried almost crumbled under my fingers. I went in.

Nobody had been there for so long that the dust had colonized it. Spiders had festooned the room, had died, and spiders had festooned the festoons. I felt my way through, coughing. A door faced me. It gave to my heel. I was in another room, more dust and sad memories of people ages before, and another door for my heel to attack. And then I was out on the roof in the soft rain and the cold wind.

The fourth storey was a mere facade, two rooms deep, with behind it the flat, leaded roof, dotted here and there with protruberances, chimneys, skylights. To my right, therefore, would be the alley, to the left the side road. But bright light shone up into the rain ahead. Another main road. I went quickly to the left and peered over the high parapet. No possibility there, the nearest building being forty feet away. Then to the right. The alleyway gap. And I saw my only chance.

The building the other side of the alley was newer than this one, and two storeys higher. And the gap was a mere ten feet. I'm very good at judging distances. I blinked the rain from my eyes and looked again. Yes, around ten feet. The parapet my side was a foot high, a foot-and-a-half across. I stood on it and looked down, and my head swam. The two buildings were sheer, the resulting perspective giving an increased illusion of height. I raised my head and looked opposite again. A yard or two to my left there was a double-sash window, open two feet at the bottom. I shuffled sideways and stood directly opposite to it.

Ten feet is not far. Put my arms above my head and I'd got about seven feet to start with. I did so. Ten feet is really very little. Seven from ten is three. It'd mean only a leap of three feet, and a good solid windowsill to cling to. Nothing to it.

The rain coursed down my face as I told myself how little it was, and a memory of that disappearing perspective almost blacked me out.

Only three feet. You simply lean forward and judge the right moment. Ten feet's nothing.

It wasn't rain, it was sweat. I glanced down and back again quickly, and realized that the time for decision was past, because I was already leaning forward, and leaning more each moment.

I don't think I cried with fear. I sprang out into nothingness, my hands reaching, found the sill, and my knees crashed down into the brickwork beneath. I groaned. My arms tore with the effort, but my toes had no purchase. I drew myself upwards, fighting for an elbow over the edge.

Then the window flew up, an arm reached under mine, and a voice said: "Easy now, sir. We've got you safe."

I was whimpering and sobbing as they drew me up, the thought of that plunge to the flagstones below suddenly choking me with terror. They were very good with me, dragging me up from my fear, setting me on my feet, dusting me down, whilst my teeth chattered and I shook from head to foot.

"Anybody got any brandy?" said a voice.

"No, no!" I shook my head violently. Brandy on an empty stomach I couldn't handle. Somebody caught my jaw and held it, and a flask clattered against my teeth. The spirit hit my throat and I choked, then it flowed into my blood. My head swam.

"Now be a good gentleman and come with us," they said, and they led me all the way down that echoing building and out into the street, and back to my own office entrance.

They all seemed to want to come and watch my defeat. They gathered silently. I did not look at their eyes. Sympathy would have broken me apart. I saw Ravat. He at least did not disguise his hatred. Maybe he knew how Toni's fate hung in the balance. I knew about Elsa's. I looked away, put my head down, and plunged towards my own building.

Anthony Brent was standing just inside the entrance. He didn't speak as I pushed past, and I didn't hear his footsteps behind as I dragged my aching body up the stairs.

The office now seemed a haven of welcome; the scattered sandwiches and crumpled bed were articles that I recognized as part of my life. My life might end there. If Elsa died, what more could there be? I sat in the chair behind my desk. I wondered what the time was.

There was a quiet cough in the doorway. My nerves jumped, associating it with Slim. But it was Anthony Brent.

"I saw you come in," he said.

"I know."

"I've been talking with the sergeant."

I waved a hand wearily. "Then I ought to throw you out."

He smiled weakly and took my gesture as an invitation to draw up the other chair.

"It's bad, isn't it?" he asked.

"It's bad."

"Is there anything I can do?"

Then I really looked at him, forcing my eyes into focus. He was nothing, you understand, no body to him, no toughness, and looking at me with his sister's expressive and soft eyes.

"You can go home and lock yourself in."

"The sergeant says the man's got your wife, and he wants to swap her for my sister."

I nodded. "Briefly put, yes."

"But he'll kill your wife," he said bluntly. He waited. I couldn't speak. "Will he kill Toni if you let him have her?"

"I don't think . . . " I couldn't sit there and look at him and talk about Toni, not with her eyes probing me. I got up quickly and went to the window. "This Petrucchi seems to want Toni to give her evidence in court. She couldn't do that if she was hurt in any way. No, I don't think he would harm her." I tried to smile. "But once he'd got her, he'd threaten to harm your wife or your child or yourself."

"So Toni herself wouldn't be in danger?"

"Not physically. Her emotions perhaps. Her mind . . . She'd be terrified."

I turned in time to see his mouth tighten. "But your wife will die," he insisted stubbornly. I could have belted him for that. I stood and watched him. He looked up. "Mr Mallin, my wife and the little girl are at the station right now. He can't reach them. That leaves me, doesn't it? And if there's only me who can be touched, then I think I've got the right to make a decision."

"What decision?" I said hoarsely.

"If you will give me the number, I'll phone this Petrucchi person for you. Tell me where Toni is, and I'll give him the address."

Who the hell did he think he was, coming there and sticking ideas under my nose? Sitting there in my chair and making preposterous suggestions.

Got a right, had he? A right to put himself in danger? He didn't owe me any favours. I wasn't going to accept any noble gestures, not when I was too weak to refuse, too stupid to accept, too shaken to control my emotions. Who was he to come and choke my throat so that I had to shout? Had to shout — oh, any old nonsense, just to shock him out of it.

"You get to hell out of here! Cheap bloody tricks. Oh sure — give you Toni's address! A pretty trick that is. You come straight here from Lew Braine, and you ask me for her address. And I'm supposed to say: friend, friend, you've saved my life. Then you'll go running back to your sergeant buddy with it. Oh no. Not me. I'm about done, but not finished. Not finished yet, clever boy."

But he remained there stubbornly, gazing into my face, not flinching, although I must have been a sight.

"The sergeant doesn't know I'm here," he said quietly, and with such sincerity that the indecision was a positive pain in my gut.

"I don't want to make choices," I said, my voice strange.

"It's me who's made the choice," he pointed out.

I could have killed him. The trouble was that I couldn't trust anybody; I was too used to bluff and counter-bluff. Sincerity completely baffled me.

"Have you got a cigarette?" I asked him.

He produced them shyly. "I don't smoke at home."

I lit up, drew the smoke in heavily, and asked: "Do you really want to help?" I was only testing him.

He nodded.

"Then — will you create a diversion for me?"

"You really don't trust me?"

"I trust you to make a diversion."

He grimaced. "It's easier to make a telephone call."

The motoring coat was too big for him, and the hat fell over his eyes.

It would fool them for perhaps thirty seconds. I was continuing with the test, allowing it to run away with me into reality.

"I want you to run towards the alley," I told him. "Not the main street. It's to the left as you go out."

"When?"

"In five minutes. Exactly."

He nodded. "I still think it'd be better . . . What's this in the pocket?"

I took the ashtray from him. He explored again. "No gun?" he asked.

"No gun, laddie. This is the real stuff. Anybody can be brave with a gun in his hand."

Then I watched him walk down the stairs, looking like shrunken and ineffectual Dave, but nevertheless probably feeling rather more confident and less terrified than I was.

I was counting on one thing. When they'd rescued me from the window I'd obviously been so scared that they'd assume I'd never try it again. They might have assumed strongly enough to have withdrawn the men from that building. So I was going to try it again. Or so I told myself.

One minute found me on the flat roof. The rain persisted. The orange glow hung in the lowering clouds. I approached the parapet and peered over.

And there was no window open. They had closed it.

My hands were clammy, my face hot. This was going to be my last chance, and my only one. Yet I could not take it. I stood on the parapet and lifted my hand to try and read my watch. But of course it had stopped earlier, and I hadn't wound it. I had no way of telling how much of the five minutes remained. And in my left hand I was still clutching the glass ashtray.

I climbed upon the parapet, and the ten feet seemed to have stretched out to twenty. Was it possible that I had already done it once? My heart hammered. I could not do it twice, certainly not with the window closed.

No — I could not. I switched the ashtray to my right hand, slightly bent my knees, and strained my ears. Any second now he'd make his run, the poor, pitiful cowardly hero that he was. He'd shame me with his courage. I'd still be standing there when he'd expended it.

Then there was a shout below and clattering heels that seemed only a foot or two below me. I had to make my move, which could only be to throw the ashtray through the lower pane, and hurl myself after it. Ten feet. You can't miss a window at that distance. I threw the ashtray.

I missed. The ashtray flew high and through the upper pane, even as I concentrated every muscle on projecting my hands towards the lower one. I made a frantic adjustment, flung up my arms, writhed, it seemed, in space, and my fingers scrambled in to lock on the central crossbar, and on to the remaining shards of the shattered glass.

I very nearly screamed. My knees came in after me and smashed against the sill. I drew them up, twisting, and my feet went through the lower pane. Was it possible that the crash could go unnoticed? But my legs were through. I swung myself down and forward, my body following my legs through the lower pane, and fell to the floor.

There was no one there. It was dark. I couldn't see what had happened to my hands, but they were hot and wet. I got to my feet and began to run. As I'd been the same way before, I could find the stairs, run down them, fall down them. Still no alarm. I could hear activity outside somewhere. It seemed that Anthony was putting up a good show. I reached the front door. Nobody was in the porch. I peered out cautiously.

This was the side road, with my own office further up, the alley in between. Around the alley there was a heaving mass of men. There were shouts and loud voices. It was more than Anthony could have caused alone. Perhaps Ravat had led his followers to the attack, fighting anything at all when the target was unclear.

But it was my chance. They were not looking my way. I turned up my hands. Blood was pouring from my palms, and in the left one I could see bone. The pain was a hot agony, which I became aware of only as I stared at the damage. I found a handkerchief, rolled it up, and clutched it hard in my left hand. I turned to run. I'd need my right hand for dialling. My legs were weak.

Then a car came from the opposite direction to the alley. I watched with curiosity as it approached, only vaguely disturbed by its rising engine note. But it was one of the big black cars. One of Petrucchi's. I wanted to contact Petrucchi — didn't I? I thought I did. Strangely, my intentions now seemed remote. The car was approaching more rapidly. I stepped out into the road and waved.

They saw me. The car wavered and

seemed to slow a little, then steadied again. It was intending to stop for me. As it came opposite, the rear door flew open and a shape was thrust out. It seemed like a limp sack of some sort. It rolled at my feet, and I saw that it was a human body.

Slowly my knees gave way from beneath me. I reached out, forcing myself like a man picking up live coals, and the blood from my hand dripped on the face as I turned it over.

It was Slim, with a neat thirty-eight hole in his forehead. What they call a mercy killing in the trade. Dainty had saved Slim from a protracted death from TB, and he'd used him as one last warning to me.

For several seconds I remained on my knees, paralysed by the shock. Then I heard a shout. I looked up. The car had ploughed through the fighting group and scattered it. Slowly I climbed to my feet and turned the other way. There was a main road out there somewhere, calling me with its orange light. I weaved as I ran on empty legs. The buildings swam each side of me. There might have been pursuit. I don't know because the blood hammered in my ears.

Then I was out into blinding light. I'd always thought the amber street-lights were restful. A phone box? Dear Lord, where had I seen a phone box? Left? I turned left.

The street was deserted. There was a little fenced square along there, a phone box against it. Then I could see it, recognize its shape if not its colour. I staggered towards it. A phone box — looking sickly grey in the orange light. I put my right hand on the door, hooked my fingers into the grip, and I couldn't open it. Sometimes they put on a strong spring. I was weak and drained. I just could not draw open the door. I whimpered and fought with it, and, with the effort, slowly my knees gave way and I slid, my right hand still hooked in the handle, slowly down to the ground. Blood ran darkly down the door.

Then a car drew up behind me. It swung round so that its headlights impaled me, and the box sprang into bright red, the shadow of my head dark again. I knew it had to be Lew Braine, and after all I wasn't going to make that call.

And, as consciousness slipped away, I was aware that I had won after all.

12

I RECOVERED consciousness in the bucket seat of Lew Braine's car, my trousers soaked with my own blood, and clutching two handkerchiefs, one in each palm. He was leaning over from the driver's seat and slapping my face.

I was vaguely aware that I should have been feeling pleased with myself, but couldn't think why.

"Mallin!" he was saying urgently. "For God's sake — "

I opened my eyes and looked at him. There was no question about his concern. Bloody hypocrite, I thought, and wondered why.

"Liven up, man," he said urgently. "There's not all that much time left."

I tried to sit up but there was no spare energy going around. My eyes refused to focus.

267

"It's finished," he told me. "There can't possibly be anything you can do now. So give me the addresses. And hurry. Where have you got Toni Brent?"

My right hand fell from my lap, and my knuckles rattled on the Krooklok he'd got down beside the seat. I absently lifted my hand to suck the pain, mumbled an address, and idly watched as he grabbed up his microphone. He snapped out the instructions, then turned and looked at me, waiting.

"And . . . " he asked.

And I grabbed up the heavy Krooklok, and smashed his radio.

"What the hell!"

But I was laughing, a revolting snicker, something that I couldn't stop until he lashed his knuckles across my mouth. I wiped my lips with his handkerchief in my right hand. He was furious about something. I don't think it was the handkerchief.

"The *other* address, Mallin."

"That's all you're getting," I told him. I'd remembered. "You've been very clever, but you made a vital mistake. Did you notice?"

"It's all been too much for you."

I was staring out of the windscreen, watching the slouching figures along the street. They drew closer, sullenly, and behind them, as a kind of back-up, lumbered the Jag and the taxi.

"Your friends are here," said Braine.

"*My* friends?"

"They must be somebody's friends."

"How d'you open this ruddy door?" I asked, struggling with it. I knew the Ravat crowd when they were roused. They had a tendency to turn over cars. "Let me out of here."

He reached across, surprised by my panic. The door opened. I tried to get out. It's easy enough to think about it, difficult to do when your legs are jelly. I stood in a kind of crippled crouch, one elbow hooked on the roof.

"What d'you think you're after?" I

269

shouted. "You're too damn late. It's all over."

Ravat thrust himself forward. He seemed to have grown a bit since I'd seen him last.

"Toni. My Toni. You're for telling the man where she is being." He was a little distraught, his English flying wild.

"I'm for telling the police. They're on their way to pick her up now." I tried to look defeated.

"Where is this they pick her up?"

I gave him the same address I'd given Braine. They stood and stared at me. The moment hung on his decision. Then he threw up his head with his hair flying. "Going to see," he shouted, and they all shouted, like an insane Greek chorus, dashed to the two vehicles, and fought their way inside.

I eased my way back into the TR6.

"You've ruined the radio," said Braine.

I watched the rabble race away. My trousers were stiff with dried blood.

"God, I feel awful." I looked sideways at him. "Thought of it yet? Your big mistake."

"Talk some sense," he said angrily. "You're wasting time."

"You followed me to the Regency on Ullswater. It was dark. You stood there in the reception — remember that red light? Everything was red. And I used their phone."

"Yes, yes, yes. I didn't notice."

"Look behind you, Lew. The phone booth. What colour is it?"

"Red, of course. You gone daft or something?"

"That's because you *know* it's red. They're always red. But does it look red? Go on, look at it. The light's orange and things will only reflect what there is to reflect. It can't look red because there's no white light, so it does its best. It looks a kind of sickly grey. I realized that, Lew. My face was inches away when you snapped on your heads, and I knew then what it meant."

"Get on with it," he growled.

But there wasn't a scrap of hurry any more. I was feeling stronger with every second.

"That phone at the Regency," I reminded him. "I thought it was white. It didn't *look* white, but it looked as white as the register did, because it was reflecting all the light there was. And that light was red, so the phone would have looked the same whether it was white or red. But it wasn't white, was it Lew? It was red."

"I don't think I really looked at it."

"No? But in my office, not so long ago, you *said* it was red. So you must have seen it as red, which meant you must have seen it in daylight, to be so positive. But when were you at the Regency in daylight? Eh? Tell me that."

"It's just a feeble idea you're flogging," he protested. But his eyes were dark with misery.

"I'll take a guess. Shall I guess that you were there the only other time

272

that the Regency became important! This morning, that would be. Go on, then," I shouted. "Deny it."

He looked away from me. "You're doing well."

"Oh yes, I'm getting along fine," I agreed. My voice was difficult to control and my mouth was light-headed. "And at that time your friend Flagg was with me at Aunt Vera's. He'd got it all fixed. He'd lost his only bit of patience and he was going to frighten me good and proper. Aunt Vera denied that she'd seen any note of the hotel's phone number. Of course she did, because it was Flagg who did that. He rigged it fine, and put on one of his acts. I had to *know* that they'd got Elsa, and you were there, the other end, standing with the receptionist to make sure I got the right answer. Two men came and took her away! My God, it sounded good, especially as two men had already been to Aunt Vera's. Only the two men at Aunt Vera's were coppers, Lew. But I didn't realize it until I thought about the red light. You were standing there in daylight, and to you it was a red phone."

I didn't understand why he didn't rage in disappointment, why his eyes held mine so steadily.

"You're so right, Mallin," he murmured. "Where did you send the inspector and those yobbos of yours?"

I laughed for a while. "He'll get a fine reception. I gave him the address where Petrucchi's staying."

"There'll be guns, you know."

"What's a few guns to that cynical slob of an inspector? Let him get roughed up a bit. He'll get his Arturo Petrucchi — but he won't have any charge against him."

"He'll have a charge all right," said Braine softly. "Dave, you guessed it all correctly. I was there. But that receptionist didn't tell any lies. He didn't need to. Two men *did* come and take your wife away. And they weren't coppers."

"Two men?" I tried to seize on the

idea. "But he couldn't!" I choked. "Not even Flagg. He couldn't have gone through with it if they really had her. Oh no, this is another bluff. You just don't give up."

"*He* doesn't. I can recognize when he's beaten, though. And he was lost from the moment they found your wife. Or he would have been lost, if I'd told him. But Flagg doesn't know, Dave. He doesn't know."

"Then — it's you!" I raised the Krooklok. He caught my wrist.

"I'm sorry, Dave. I played for the one big break, but it needed luck. And I didn't have any. You noticed the mistake about the phone. Now, *that's* when the luck ran out."

"Oh Christ, you rotten bastard."

"I told you, I owe . . . where d'you think you're going?" He reached over and clamped his hand on my arm.

"There's a phone box out there . . . the station . . . get a message through."

He shook his head. "It's out of

order. Somebody's got at it with a two-inch nail."

They were everywhere! "Then what're you sitting here for?" I screamed at him. "Can't you drive this thing!"

But he was already moving down the road. What was the matter with me, my head swimming, my brain out of focus, and sobbing like that?

"Fasten your belt," he said grimly.

But how could I do that with two hands so cut about? I rocked in the seat, shaken from side to side as he slid the corners.

The Petrucchi house was a good fifteen miles away. It gave us chance to catch up; or would have done if I hadn't wasted so much of it gloating on my clever bit of detection.

"We'd got a man standing by," he said, glancing at me.

"What for? What'd you have a man for?"

"In case you didn't head for your wife's aunt's house."

"Got it covered." Heavens, hadn't

they got it all covered! "Can't you drive any faster?"

"I can wreck the engine."

"Then wreck the bloody thing."

He tried, but that engine has a big heart. I crouched forward, urging him on frantically, but there was no sign ahead of cars racing in the same direction, and even when we turned in to the lane we had not caught them. My heart sank.

The action had started. Flagg, aware that Toni might be restrained by a group of my thuggish friends, had arrived expecting trouble. He had not expected pistol shots. They crackled out as we came to a burning halt just beyond the group of cars. The Ravat transport was parked further down.

"Round the back!" I shouted as we scrambled out.

In the night air, open to the weeping sky, the pistols sounded innocuous, like snapping twigs. A few stray bullets were not going to stop Flagg on the verge of triumph. I heard his roaring voice, and somewhere a plaintive wail that I recognized as a muted battle song.

"The back!" But I could hardly stay on my feet. Braine put a hand to my arm. The twigs rustled to a passing shot, and shapes blundered all around me. Together we ran round the side of the house as a window shattered. A pistol cracked twice. Flagg howled on a descending note and the front door crashed in at his flying progress.

They'd built a verandah on the back, all glass and a corrugated plastic roof. I was panting. "Give me a bunk up."

Braine protested: "Your hands!"

"Give me a shove," I snarled at him. "You owe *me*, Lew." And he heaved me up to the roof.

"What about me?" he cried.

"Use the dustbin."

I wasn't going to wait for him. There was a window partly open. I jerked it fully wide and fell through. I was on a landing. I peered down the stairs as Ravat flew in through a window into the hall, his arms cradling his head, and squashed a gunman against the wall.

"Elsa!"

The din was now overwhelming. I thought I heard her voice. Was sure of it. "David! I'm here."

It came from behind a door at the far end. There was a whole length of landing in which to gain momentum. I threw myself forward, shoulder down, and the door remained like rock. I thought my teeth had fallen out as I slowly collapsed to the floor. Then Lew Braine's heel shot past my head, and the door flew open.

It was not as I'd visualized it, Dave throwing his mighty and protective arms around her shoulders. It was Elsa bending over me, elegant even now in her light tweed suit, and murmuring, "Poor David. Oh, you poor dear." It was me levering myself painfully up the door-frame, hand over hand, my mouth open and gasping for air, and looking beyond Elsa's shoulder to see Dainty slowly rising from a chair in the far corner of the room, my Colt in his hand and a beatific smile of welcome on his face.

Lew Braine went for him. Dainty watched him come, and put two neat holes in his chest, and then he smiled at us again. I could not move. There was a roaring sound in my ears, like the pound of a rampaging herd up the stairs. The gun levelled between my eyes, then I was trampled into the floor and Elsa was flung aside, and Ravat saw that he was facing another of those pitiful men who stood between him and Toni.

And Dainty had not, after all, cleaned the gun, not even checked it, or he'd have known he'd used up its five shots. The firing pin clicked on to nothing, so that Ravat had no difficulty in plucking Dainty from his feet. Then he proceeded to sculpt him into a more acceptable shape. I heard cracking sounds and Dainty's screams went on and on as I crawled over to Lew Braine.

He was dead. Elsa touched my arm.

Her face was distorted with horror. I got to my feet and went over to Ravat. He still wasn't satisfied with the result.

"It's all right," I shouted into his ear. "Toni's safe. She's safe. Put him down."

He allowed Dainty to crumple down at his feet. He spat on Dainty's face with contempt. I turned to Elsa.

"Let's get out of here."

I had to get clear before the others, because there were things to be done. She helped me along the landing. I peered over, at Flagg in the hall like a trapped bull, his shoulders down to the darts and looking round for more trouble, as the one with the goatee crashed his splendid instrument to pieces on Flagg's head. The Oriental gentleman was practising his chops on Arturo Petrucchi, already unconscious and wedged against the banister.

We quietly moved through the turmoil and out into the front garden. Now there were no more pistol shots.

Cries of surrender, yes. Howls of distress. We walked away from it.

"Where's the car?" said Elsa.

We paused. "Did they hurt you?"

She shook her head. "They didn't hurt me." She glanced at my hands, then looked away. "But they hurt you."

"It was me did that. We'll use Flagg's car," I said. "You'd better drive."

I looked at my watch while the doors were still open. Five to five. I still hadn't wound it.

"Nearly twelve," said Elsa, interpreting the gesture.

He'd left the keys dangling in the ignition. Or rather, his driver had. I'd never seen Flagg driving his own car, and wondered why.

"I don't know where we are." Elsa looked round. "Which is the way home?"

"We're not going home," I told her, and I directed her in the right direction for the station.

"But your hands . . . "

"Never mind my hands."

"And David . . . " She looked pitifully at me. "I don't feel too well." Well, she wouldn't would she?

"Elsa, love," I said, "I know how you feel. But they'll give you coffee at the station, and if you're lucky a sandwich, and you can relax there. Because that nasty big inspector is going to want a statement from you, and you might as well get it over and done with."

And the nasty, big inspector might even be grateful, because he'd got Petrucchi now, got him for kidnapping and his henchman for murder, and very conveniently he'd got a dead sergeant who could carry the burden of guilt for the near-disaster.

He might even be grateful enough to allow me to keep the thousand quid Petrucchi had paid me.

"Elsa," I said, "where's the Rover?"

She drew the Cortina into the station yard. I directed her to park it beside Camille's.

"In the car park at the Regency," she

said. "At Ullswater."

"There's a lot of money in it."

"David!" She drew on the handbrake, leaned over, cupped my harried face in her hands, and kissed me tenderly. "It was so thoughtful of you. You knew I'd need spending money — but how very generous of you! You should see what I've got in the back of the Rover. Oh, I've had such a glorious time!"

I said hollowly: "You seem to be feeling better now."

13

THERE was no longer a guard in the station yard, and the station itself, when we entered by the rear door, seemed nearly deserted. I drew Elsa along until we found the desk sergeant, who summoned a couple of WPCs, and there was a great fuss over Elsa. They took her into a rest-room.

I turned. "Is there anybody who could look at my hands?"

Well, there was, because the police surgeon had just driven in, warned by radio that he'd have work to do very shortly. He unclenched my fists and removed the wadded rags.

"Stitches," he said, shaking his head. "Just plaster for now — huh?"

And it was while he was doing this that I looked away — couldn't bear the sight — and saw Anthony Brent standing in the corridor and watching me through the open door.

"You did well," I said.

His face was swollen, his lower lip thick. "I came for my wife and the kid. Maybe I can take them home now."

"You could," I agreed. I thanked the doctor. "It's all over now. But you could do something for me first."

"Give you back the coat?" He began to take it off.

"That and something else. Have you got your car?"

"It's outside."

"Then take me to pick up mine. Then we'll go and pick up your sister."

"Yes," he said. "Yes." Maybe his sore mouth precluded a smile. "I'd like that."

The Porsche was exactly as I'd left it, and the district seemed now strangely deserted.

"I'll follow you?" he asked, and I nodded, and "Here?" he asked when we drew up, and I nodded again.

It was Toni who opened the door.

"Anthony!" she screamed, and threw herself into his arms. "David!" cried Ruby, and she too opened her arms, and for a few moments I was lost to the world, somewhere enveloped in her vast joy and affection.

"Oh, it's been so splendid!" said Toni, when we'd emerged. "Do I really have to go, David?"

"Ravat is dying to see you."

"And have I got things to tell him!" she said. "He doesn't *dream* about colour. He's not living. I've been working in oils. Anthony, isn't this sensational? What you can do on canvas!"

It hadn't been a joke. There she was, Ruby Streiss in the nude, a vast rump either trying to get into or out of a bath.

I nodded agreement. "It's an effect," I agreed, "that Ravat could never achieve in wrought iron."

So, with Ruby's shouts from her window for Toni to come again, and soon, we drove away and back to the station, Toni clutching her masterpiece. She was in Anthony's car. I followed.

Anthony left his in the street, but I parked the Porsche in the yard, tail in to the offices. When I got inside it was obvious that the first contingents of police and captives were arriving. The damages to the police were remarkably small, considering. It was not clear whether the Ravat crowd were amongst the captives or the heroes. When they saw Toni there was no restraining them, whichever it was. Anthony, caught in the crush, was apparently thought to have been her rescuer. They pounded him so enthusiastically that he was almost down on his knees, beaming and almost in tears. Then he forced his way out of it, because his wife and the little girl were standing waiting for him. Mrs Brent was trying to be unencouraging. But I mean, you can't be too severe when your man's obviously the man of the moment.

Ravat was roaring in delight at the painting. He waved it over his head.

"Let's have some quiet here," Flagg bellowed.

The silence was abrupt. He stood by the desk, torn and dishevelled, his eyes red, his face grim, but his head was back. Flagg had won. He'd won, yes he had, and as an added bonus they'd found Emilio Sarturo crouching under the stairs. Not, mind you, that Flagg would know what to charge him with, but he'd think of something. Flagg always did.

I touched Toni's elbow. "I'd like you to identify the car."

Her eyes were huge. "But I did."

"You described it, and they found one that fits. Later, perhaps?" I asked, aware that soon she'd be very busy.

I looked in on Elsa. It was she who'd provide the central evidence against Arturo, but I was hoping to get her away before they started on her, or we'd be there all night. Maybe Flagg would be prepared to allow her to come back the next day. He owed me a favour or two.

Elsa was surrounded by policemen, none interested in statements, and she was glowing in the spotlight of their interest. I went out again. The corridor was a chaos of shouting coppers, of crooks spread on benches, with Ravat still there demanding his rights as a citizen. I edged through it, got to the rear door, and breathed deeply of the night air out in the yard.

I looked round. The setting was perfect. The yard occupied a junction of two roads, and had the benefit of four orange street-lamps. I needed no torch for what I wanted to do.

Everybody seemed to have forgotten that I'd been employed to help Camille, and though the method suggested had not been acceptable, the contract was still valid. I had already probed Lew Braine with an idea about Camille's car. It was time to test it.

But I couldn't test it on Camille's car, because of the key wedged in the lock. What I wanted to check was a non-wedged key, and the only car to try that on was Flagg's, which was fortunately the same model.

I reached inside and took his keys from the ignition lock. Two keys on a ring. I assumed they were duplicates, because on that model Cortina you only need one key for the lot. But one key was for the ignition, and one for the boot. I opened the boot and it sprang up, impelled by its spring. I pulled it down towards me and held it level, and tried the firmness of the key in its lock.

This was a new key, but all the same it wouldn't stay in firmly enough to take any sort of strain. But even so, I wasn't certain. I needed string, and there was string already wrapped around the key in Camille's boot. I unfastened it.

Now, this wasn't as easy as it sounds. You know what wet string is like, and my hands weren't exactly delicate instruments. I finally untied it, and tried several thicknesses over the key in Flagg's car. And as I'd guessed, when

I jerked the boot lid a few times, the key worked out of the lock.

Five minutes later I re-entered the building, my hands sore and my stomach feeling rough. I went to find Elsa. Her escort was down to two. I said: "Excuse me, gentlemen, may I talk to my wife?"

"Oh," she said, "are we ready to leave?" Vaguely disappointed.

I tried to smile. She caught my mood, apologized around, and followed me quickly into the corridor.

"What is it, David?"

"I want you to go and sit in the car. I've got the Porsche outside."

"But I was quite comfortable in there."

"There's something I want you to do."

"Oh dear," she said, peering in to my face. "You've gone all funny again."

I took her by the arm and led her out into the yard. I put her behind the wheel.

"Are we going to make a quick

getaway?" she asked solemnly, fastening the seat belt.

"I hope it won't come to that." I told her what I wanted her to do. Then I went back inside, where the desk sergeant caught my eye. "Mr Flagg's looking for you."

"And I'm looking for him."

Flagg was in the interrogation-room talking to Toni. I could see it was informal, because he had Anthony and his family in there. He turned as I came in.

It was the first time we'd been face to face since he'd left me at the office. All the tension of the past few days was streaming out and leaving him spent. His eyes were deep and haunted, his shoulders slack.

"You know?" he said.

I nodded. "I had a talk with Lew Braine."

There was a brief flicker of pain in his eyes, then it passed. "Does it help if I say I'm sorry?"

I didn't know whether it helped

293

or not. With a sudden gesture he produced a piece of crumpled paper, straightened it, and held it out. I took it from him.

It was the top sheet from Aunt Vera's phone pad, and on it was the phone number of the Regency. I looked up.

"If anything had happened to Elsa, you know I'd have killed you?"

"I was quite unaware that they'd really — "

"But all the same I'd have done it."

"I had to have my witness." He tried painfully to smile. "I was under pressure. I acted on impulse."

"Some day," I said, "you'll act on impulse once too often."

He seemed to recoil, and then steadied. "I . . . you interrupted an interrogation," he said stiffly.

"You were just talking. But you may not need Toni's evidence, after all. Come outside, I want to show you something."

He hesitated.

"You too, Toni," I said. "It shouldn't take long."

Then I walked with confidence back to the yard, and as usually happens when you act with confidence, they all followed me.

I had read how it was done. This big-headed detective gathers round him all the protagonists and suspects, and delivers a resumé of events and an unanswerable final exposure of the criminal. Well, all I can say is that he hasn't tried doing it in a draughty police yard at three in the morning, with the rain starting again, and not a flaming protagonist in sight. I did my best. They wanted to get back inside, Flagg impatient, the desk sergeant merely nosey, Anthony and family only there in order not to let Toni out of their sight again. And me.

"Toni," I said, "can you now identify the car? The light's about the same as it was that night."

"Oh yes," she said. "But I do think

. . . well, the boot lid was a bit wider open."

"They've had the string off and put it back again," I said blandly. I turned to Flagg. "So there you are."

"I'm not anywhere," he said angrily. "What's so different?"

"Well now, haven't you worried about it — about why anyone even vaguely connected with the Petrucchis would use Camille's car?" He stared at me. "Doesn't it strike you as fantastic that whoever it was would load an empty beer keg — and that obviously from the back of Camille's club — into the boot in order to go out and do this thing?"

"Well of course," he said defensively. "But they're not great brains, Mallin. And that wasn't the point."

"No," I agreed. "It wasn't. The point was to use it to apply pressure to Arturo."

"Then why're you making such a fuss about it?"

I looked beyond him. One or two of

the others had come out to see what was going on. I went on, with more strength to my voice.

"I've just told you how unlikely it is that this car was used. But there's something else. The boot was partly open and string was holding it down. The car's a Cortina, and there's thousands of 'em. So how could it have been identifiable if the boot *hadn't* been open? And yet you seem to think that somebody would go out to run down your wife in a car in *that* condition, when he could . . . "

I stepped forward quietly, my penknife open in my hand, and slashed the string through. The boot lid flew up.

" . . . have done this," I said. I turned the keg over on its side and rolled it into the deepest part of the boot. I slammed the boot lid shut.

"But he didn't," said Flagg.

"No," I agreed. "He did not. But he went even further than that. Camille had left his key in. One key, mind. And *that* key was used in the ignition lock.

There's a different key in the boot lock, a foreigner to that lock, and wedged in. It'd need to be wedged in, because the proper key would have worked its way out. So that has got to mean that whoever used that car also used his own car key to wedge into that boot lock. He did all that, all those things, when none of them was necessary, the key only being there to hold the boot lid open."

"All right," said Flagg. "I'll agree with you, if it'll make you happy. Now come inside and we'll discuss it."

"We'll discuss it here," I said, because after all I was the only one with a coat on. "I'm trying to tell you that this wasn't the car that ran down your wife."

"It's got dents — "

"Certainly. They could have been put in, by somebody who'd go to all the other trouble. There didn't have to be dents, but they look good. Camille claims his car was stolen. I believe it was. But everything I've said leads to one conclusion, and that is that it was stolen in order to make it look like the real killer car, and that means it was stolen *after* your wife was run down."

He breathed deeply. "Fine, Mallin. I get your point. I had a poor case against the Petrucchis, but you're strengthening it. Perhaps they were more clever than I thought, used another car, then planted this one, knowing I'd never make it stick . . . "

"No."

"Come inside," he pleaded.

"I've got more to say. The other car, Flagg, the one that really did it, that's where you're going to trip up. It's been worrying me, because, you see, it must have looked just as Toni described it, otherwise this one wouldn't have been rigged the same. And do you realize what that implies? Eh?"

He didn't. He offered no assistance.

"It had me really bogged down," I admitted. "The first thing is the boot lid. I mean, if the real murder car had its boot tied with string, and partly open, then it follows that the string had to be hooked over something. And as I've said, the key designed for that lock would have worked its way out. Another foreign key? Oh, I don't think so. In just the same way, it's most unlikely there was another beer keg holding it open. But when you come to wonder *why* the boot was tied at all, then you come to thinking about busted locks, and you wonder whether perhaps one of our lovely little kiddie-winkies might not have got at it with a two-inch nail. That'd explain both things, why the boot lid was open, and how it was tied."

"Oh Lord, Mallin, I'm going in if you're not." And Flagg turned away.

I tried it on the desk sergeant, who at least seemed patient, and perhaps not quite so cold.

"And I mean, if the lock on the murder car was busted, then it would've had to be repaired, and damn quick, and a repair means a new key, because a new lock would've had to be put in."

I didn't think Flagg had gone far, but I couldn't see him.

"Go on, sir," said the sergeant, who I was sure would make super in time.

"Well, I mean," I said, "if somebody did a swap of the cars it'd have to be somebody who knew that the Petrucchi crowd had a car that fitted the description." He nodded. "But the really interesting thing is that he should have known what that description was. It was Toni who said it was a dark-grey Cortina, and she'd said it at the station here, and yet shortly afterwards Camille's grey car was stolen and rigged to fit the exact description. Sergeant, it means . . . Flagg, are you there? You want to hear this. Link it all with the fact that we're looking for somebody with *two* keys for his Cortina, one for his ignition and a new one for his boot lock . . ."

I waved towards the Porsche and gave Elsa the prearranged signal. It should have been a startling climax to my hard work — but nothing happened.

I ran to the Porsche. Elsa, poor lamb, was fast asleep. I reached past her, and she snapped awake at the same time as the headlights.

They shone stark white right on the car that Toni had identified a few minutes before. It was the maroon Cortina that belonged to Flagg.

At the same time I realized that I'd just shown, by considered argument, that the person who had stolen Camille's car might still have Camille's ignition key in his pocket. Flagg proved me to be correct. He started Camille's engine, jerked the gear into reverse, and did a big sweep to bring the nose of the grey Cortina in line with the open gateway. I shouted and began to run. The whole thing was futile. Where could he go? Then he engaged first and got moving to nowhere.

But I'd startled Elsa awake. She heard me shout, saw me running, knew I was trying to stop the Cortina. The Porsche engine sprang into life and Elsa, bless her, with that precision with which she manages to settle things, omitted to recall that she was not in one of her own cars, and shot across the yard. Maybe the acceleration was more than she'd expected. She caught that Cortina squarely in the side, squashed its door in, picked it up and hurled it against the corner of the wall, and everything stopped with a horrid crunch and an agonized silence. I ran shouting to the Porsche.

She was fine. Steam rose from the crushed radiator under the crumpled bonnet, and one front wheel leered up at the sky. But Elsa was unharmed. She was even delighted. She's always pleased to help me when needed.

I got her out of the car. "You're all right?"

She threw back her head. "He nearly got away."

"I should have warned him about you, Elsa."

Flagg was trapped by his leg in the crumpled Cortina, in agony but not willing to admit it. I wrenched open the wrecked door, afraid of fire, but there was no sign of it. Men came running and the sergeant shouted instructions. But it would need flame-cutters to get him out. They sent for the necessary men. Where was Ravat, I wondered, as a passing thought.

I bent over Flagg. His voice was hard and sharp. "I knew what my wife was doing to me, Mallin. I couldn't live with it. Deceiving me with another man! It was like a knife in my guts."

"I know. You've got your pride."

He'd said it all, there at Aunt Vera's. He hadn't been talking about Elsa and me, he'd been talking about his wife and himself. And even then he'd used his own pain to forward his ends.

"It went on and on," he said. "Months. I couldn't stop it. I knew, you see, but I didn't know who. Until recently. Then I found which bus she came home on each time, back-checked it, waited at bus stops . . ." He groaned, I thought with pain.

"They'll be here soon."

He ignored it. "And then, that night, I saw. She got out of . . . *his* car. I was mad with fury. I don't know what I wanted to do. Strike at her somehow — and all I had with me was the car. I didn't mean . . . I don't know."

"And you saw at last who she'd been meeting?"

"It was Lew Braine. My own sergeant!"

I wished they'd hurry with that equipment. A bit more of this and I'd find myself enjoying his pain. It explained why Flagg had used Lew Braine so mercilessly, why Lew had suffered it, knowing why, realizing every time he spoke to his inspector that Flagg hated him. But had he known that Flagg had killed his wife? Surely not. He'd driven away before it happened. But he'd felt Flagg's hatred, and he'd accepted it as his due.

"And you decided to fake Camille's car?" I asked.

"I heard the young lady's inaccurate description of my car, and I realized what it fitted. My chance, Mallin, my chance!"

I turned away, sickened by that poor, wretched bitter man, who'd been able to use his own burning emotions throughout in a cold and deadly plan to trap his enemies, and at the same time to dodge the consequences of his own crime.

And then I remembered Lew Braine, tortured to a point where he'd even risk Elsa's life, and I turned back savagely.

"And while you were working on all your insane objects, Flagg, you missed the main point of it all. Don't you realize what Petrucchi wanted? All the way through he insisted that Toni should be allowed to give her evidence. But not identify Camille's car. It *means* something, Flagg. If he'd removed her you'd have had no witness, but all you'd have done then would've been to apply for more time. You'd have gone on and on. But if she'd altered her evidence, your case would have failed."

"His brother . . . " he said weakly.

"No! Do you imagine he cares one tiny jot for his brother? No, Flagg, if she'd said that Camille's car wasn't the right one, you'd have had to release the car, not Camille. It was the car Arturo wanted, *this* car, Flagg, which you've had under guard all this time. Look at it, remember that Camille was intending to go to London, and that Emilio Sarturo came up here to see what was going on."

I tore at the door lining, which was cracked and broken. It didn't do my hands any good, but it helped my mood no end. The lining fell away, revealing the metal framework. I plunged in my hand and withdrew a plastic bag. Sheer luck of course, but it had to be there somewhere. I shook it in Flagg's tormented face.

"Heroin!" I shouted. "It was here in the car. Ready packed. And you, you poor, stupid, egotistical maniac — you missed it."

And then at last I turned away. The

men thrust me aside, trundling in with their trolley of gas bottles.

"Please," said Ravat. "I can help?"

I shook my head. "You can't help him."

Elsa took my arm. "Come away, David, you're upset."

And I listened to myself laughing. "Away where? The Dolomite's at home, the Rover's in Cumberland, and you've wrecked the Porsche."

But Toni insisted that Anthony would drive us home, and there began one of those complicated discussions as to who would take whom where and when.

I sat down slowly on the station steps. Toni said:

"David, you needn't have gone to all that trouble, you know."

I looked up. "Trouble?"

"I learned a lot from Ruby. All about light and colours. I knew how I'd made the mistake, and I'd have changed my evidence, anyway. I knew a maroon car would look dark-grey in orange light."

"But I didn't," I said. "It took me quite a while to find out."

Though when you come to think of it, I'd got no excuse, because both the Porsche and the Dolomite cars are red, and I'd been driving them around for days in orange light, never noticing how different they looked.

But you don't notice, do you, unless it's shoved under your nose?

Elsa said: "Anthony's going to run his family home, then drop Mr Ravat and Toni, and we'll . . ."

But I don't recall the actual sequence of the journey, because I fell asleep in the car, and it was around three the following afternoon that I recovered enough to remember that five hundred of that money was really George Coe's, and that I'd promised Toni five hundred to change her evidence — and she had.

"Did you spend it *all*, Elsa?" I groaned.

A FOOT IN THE GRAVE
Bruce Marshall

About to be imprisoned and tortured in Buenos Aires, John Smith escapes, only to become involved in an aeroplane hijacking.

DEAD TROUBLE
Martin Carroll

Trespassing brought Jennifer Denning more than she bargained for. She was totally unprepared for the violence which was to lie in her path.

HOURS TO KILL
Ursula Curtiss

Margaret went to New Mexico to look after her sick sister's rented house and felt a sharp edge of fear when the absent landlady arrived.

THE DEATH OF ABBÉ DIDIER
Richard Grayson

Inspector Gautier of the Sûreté investigates three crimes which are strangely connected.

NIGHTMARE TIME
Hugh Pentecost

Have the missing major and his wife met with foul play somewhere in the Beaumont Hotel, or is their disappearance a carefully planned step in an act of treason?

BLOOD WILL OUT
Margaret Carr

Why was the manor house so oddly familiar to Elinor Howard? Who would have guessed that a Sunday School outing could lead to murder?

THE DRACULA MURDERS
Philip Daniels

The Horror Ball was interrupted by a spectral figure who warned the merrymakers they were tampering with the unknown.

THE LADIES
OF LAMBTON GREEN
Liza Shepherd

Why did murdered Robin Colquhoun's picture pose such a threat to the ladies of Lambton Green?

CARNABY
AND THE GAOLBREAKERS
Peter N. Walker

Detective Sergeant James Aloysius Carnaby-King is sent to prison as bait. When he joins in an escape he is thrown headfirst into a vicious murder hunt.

MUD IN HIS EYE
Gerald Hammond

The harbourmaster's body is found mangled beneath Major Smyle's yacht. What is the sinister significance of the illicit oysters?

THE SCAVENGERS
Bill Knox

Among the masses of struggling fish in the *Tecta*'s nets was a larger, darker, ominously motionless form . . . the body of a skin diver.

DEATH IN ARCADY
Stella Phillips

Detective Inspector Matthew Furnival works unofficially with the local police when a brutal murder takes place in a caravan camp.